THE DARK WATERS

BOOKS IN THE ARGOSY LIBRARY:

GOLDEN RIVER: THE COMPLETE
ADVENTURES OF BEN QUORN, VOLUME 1
TALBOT MUNDY

LADY OF THE NIGHT WIND
VARICK VANARDY

KING OF THE EXILES
THOMSON BURTIS

FOR A POINT OF HONOR: THE COMPLETE
CASES OF RIORDAN, VOLUME 2
VICTOR MAXWELL

THE DARK WATERS
WILLIAM CORCORAN

MURDER WITHOUT MOTIVE: THE COMPLETE
CASES OF SHOW-ME McGEE, VOLUME 1
FREDERICK C. DAVIS

MURDER IN THE NUDIST CLUB
FRED MACISAAC

GORILLA CARGO: THE COMPLETE
ADVENTURES OF McNALLY, VOLUME 1
RICHARD WORMSER

GREEN MAMBA: THE COMPLETE
CASES OF DAFFY DILL, VOLUME 2
RICHARD B. SALE

THE SILENCER MYSTERY: THE COMPLETE
CASES OF GILLIAN HAZELTINE, VOLUME 3
GEORGE F. WORTS

THE DARK WATERS

WILLIAM CORCORAN

ILLUSTRATED BY
SAMUEL CAHAN

POPULAR PUBLICATIONS · 2024

TABLE OF CONTENTS

THE DARK WATERS

*Dex Ward, private bodyguard, found
more danger in the rackets of New
York gangsters than mere gun-play*

1

UNPROFESSIONAL BODYGUARD

IT WAS BETWEEN show opening and show break, the hour of evening's lull, of quiet on Times Square. But to the eyes of the man from Mars it would still have seemed riot and confusion. It was but the false calm in the storm center of the cyclone. The high tides of humanity, past the flood, paused before the onrushing midnight ebb. The sidewalks still were crowded, barkers chanted their spiels, police whistles shrilled, auctioneers bellowed, auto horns swore and threatened, a myriad million lights blazed and flickered.

Before the entrance to the Excella Theater—High Class Burlesque, Morris Weiss, Producer—Dex Ward diligently earned his daily bread. He wore a flamboyant blue and gold uniform never before seen on land or sea, and he exhorted the passing throng to enter and bear witness to the assertion on the marquee that Morris Weiss' high class burlesque was incomparably extravagant and gorgeous and refined.

Dex Ward was thirty-two, six feet two inches, one hundred and ninety pounds. He had a past that included sculling, wrestling, boxing, marksmanship, and private detective agency experience (for which he had strong distaste), all of which had combined, oddly, to place him on Times Square. He had found himself a burlesque barker by no design of his own. And for lack of better immediate occupation, he barked and spieled and displayed the blue and gold uniform with an amount of ardor completely satisfying to Morris Weiss, whose worried soul found comfort in the presence before his box office of six feet two of stalwart male of the caliber of Dexter Ward. Morris Weiss was a smart man.

A small car pulled up at a vacant place at the curb close to the Excella Theater about ten o'clock this evening. Two men got out. They conferred a moment with the driver, who remained at the wheel. Then the two, undersized, shifty-eyed, young, strolled over the crowded sidewalk to

*Dex's guns
roared defiance*

the Excella box office. The box office was a frail, composition board booth situated almost out on the sidewalk, the better to entice the customers. A wooden-faced, elaborate-coiffured blonde dealt out the tickets.

The pair studied the prices displayed above the box office. Then they talked with the blonde, crowding the window together. In the slack hour they were the only

The wheels spun desperately

applicants for admission. The discussion seemingly struck a snag, for the blonde took on an expression of wide-eyed distress, and the pair became inaudibly vehement about something.

Dex Ward eyed the scene, frowning a little, barely pausing in his chanted appeal to the world. He halted, debated, caught the eye of the blonde, and advanced upon the box office.

"Butso!" snapped one of the pair at the window, using the cryptic word of alarm peculiar to New York. He backed away a little; the other remained at the window.

Then Dex Ward saw the .32 revolver in the hand of the man at the window, pointed at the blonde, and a split second later, another similar weapon in the hand of the one who had backed away. The latter gun was trained squarely on the center of the handsome uniform. Its holder took strategic position alongside a foyer pillar, which concealed him from the embarrassing view of the crowd on the street.

Ward called to the blonde, "Hold everything!" Then he shouted, "Hey—*you!*"

The fellow at the window, viciously demanding action on the part of the frozen blonde, spun on his heels instinctively at the summons, started to the ends of his brilliantined hair. The gun came with him, leveled, deadly.

Ward slapped the gun quickly, grabbed him. The gun exploded, chiseling a flake of inlay neatly out of the flooring. Ward lifted the stunned fellow clear from the ground, heaved him, as he might a medicine ball, squarely at the other gunman. He followed up, charging both.

A CROWD OF onlookers, frozen in their tracks, stared—then as another gunshot echoed in the foyer, scattered in full panic. Dex Ward had the scene, the situation all to himself. The blonde set up a rhythmic series of piercing screams.

There was a rather vicious delighted smile on Ward's normally pleasant, strong face. The pair had no chance, and he knew it. And since they, with their guns, afforded such excellent opportunity for commendable and violent action, he took full advantage. He shook them. He grabbed at flailing gun hands, and flailed them a little more. He sent one weapon flying so far that it smashed a small pane of glass in an inner door. He cracked down on the floor so hard with another that the revolver slid harmlessly from limp, paralyzed fingers. He hauled both erect by the scruff of the neck, and he brought both heads together in violent, stunning collision. He dragged the pair close to the wall, propped them up, and watched them slide slowly, help-lessly to seated collapse on the floor.

Then he reseated his military cap squarely on his head, adjusted his slightly disheveled uniform, and yelled into the foyer, "Hey—Weiss! Come on out. All finished. Take care of this."

A small office door popped open, and Weiss popped out, short, fat, bald, perspiring, wide-eyed. He took one look, and popped back in again to telephone the police, a quite superfluous but doubtless prudent thing to do.

Ward, standing guard over the suffering pair of bandits, kicked the nearby gun into the foyer out of harm's way. He glanced out over the deserted sidewalk at the crowd lining the traffic island curbing—at what they judged a safe distance. To one side of the theater he noticed a single man standing alone, the only one who had not stampeded. His gaze passed the man, then suddenly snapped back full upon him, intently.

The man smiled slightly. He was a tall, dark-eyed man of Ward's age, beautifully groomed in rather somber, inconspicuous clothes, dark gray top coat, derby, black shoes, walking stick.

Ward and the man stared at each other for a full half minute, and in their eyes a myriad urgent questions formed and found no immediate answer. The man came forward. He ignored the captive pair. The smile was gone, and there was a quizzical, sardonic look on his lean, handsome, somehow predatory face.

"My God," he said, and he sounded shocked, "what on earth are you doing in that monkey suit?"

Ward took a deep breath. He grinned. "It's a living, Tev."

"A living? You?"

"Sure! Hell, who cares? I'm seeing life, excitement, the bright lights, the Great White Way. You ought to see the girls go by."

Teverson did not grin. His eyes narrowed. "Girls, my eye! After the women you've known? I'll bet you haven't spent a dollar on a beautiful woman in months."

To Ward, the mere mention was a sudden piercing thing. "Make it years. But they'll wait, Tev."

Teverson was sharp. "Don't be an ass! What are you doing in that uniform?"

"Necessity. Ever hear of it?"

"Get rid of it," snapped Teverson. "Dispose of this pair of punks you slapped down, and get into your clothes."

Ward arched skeptical brows. "What then?"

"You do as I say. Get out of the monkey suit and come along with me."

WARD SOBERED, STUDYING him. Charity? No, not in that tone of voice. Command was in it, and much money, and something else. Something unfathomable.

Ward said, "Here comes Weiss. I'll turn this over to him. I'll be five minutes changing. Wait here."

And so it was, and Dex Ward went away with Teverson, whom he had not seen in four eventful years, and the screeching, almost tearful protests of Morris Weiss were wasted on the callous Times Square air.

They walked in silence, pushing through the crowd, and Dex Ward's mind was a kaleidoscope of many-faceted recollection, of misgiving and of wonder. Teverson!

The memory of glittering years was full of the man, fascinating, inscrutable. In those years when puzzles about life or money were small concerns to a young scion of much wealth, when misgiving and wonder were nonexistent, Dex Ward had rather taken him for granted. They'd both been mavericks, alone, without families.

They had played and worked and traveled together, shared dollars and drinks and dates impartially. College first. Then Europe. Munich, Cologne, Berlin. Teverson taking his music lightly, brilliantly. Ward exhausting the architectural history of all Europe. So unlike each other, so perfectly a team!

How credulous they, thinking it was to last forever. Dex Ward had relied confidently on his luck, his boundless energy, and on the ample trust fund established by his late father, who had started life as a lumberjack in Michigan timber and fought his roaring way through life to a fortune in forests and pulp mills. Of these reliances only Ward's energy remained now.

Dex Ward wondered. By the look of him, Teverson had suffered little. And Ward could understand that. Teverson, in his own peculiar way both ruthless and fairly unscrupulous, was not the man to permit himself to suffer.

That very fact had been the issue on which their friend-

ship crashed four years ago. It was in Paris. An episode still
unpleasant in Dex Ward's eyes. A vain, truculent and ridic-
ulously self-assured young man, with all he possessed in
his pocket, had covetously tried to buck Teverson at bacca-
rat. His unbridled tongue was taunting, foul. Ward would
simply have knocked him down and silenced him. Teverson gave him all the rope he wanted, and blandly took him
for every cent he possessed, playing as he always gambled,
with infinite skill and certainty. Then, dropping the mask,
he had slapped the appalled young man's pallid face and
kicked him out into the night, penniless and stranded and
in tears. His laughter of satisfaction was sardonic, unpit-
ying.

Ward did not like the incident. The fellow deserved
it, but it seemed a little unnecessary, a little too easy and
deliberate. The consequences for them were a few extra
francs—for the young fool who lost, perhaps tragic. Dex
Ward demurred and made known his mind.

The result was startling and unexpected. Teverson had
blazed his contempt for weaklings, for sentimental pity, for
sympathy with fools. The contempt carried a personal sting,
and Ward flashed back. There was a quarrel. It lost all sight
of its original issue, it flamed out of a brew of months and
years in the making. It was no mere clash of the moment,
it became a contest to the finish between utterly divergent
opinions, philosophies, ultimate beliefs.

IT ENDED ABRUPTLY when Dex Ward, goaded beyond
endurance, stretched his friend unconscious on the floor
of the hotel room with one raging blow. Ward packed his
things and was gone before Teverson came to. He caught

the first boat for home, and did not see or hear from Teverson again—until this extraordinary and eventful evening.

Teverson led the way to a booth in the rear of the famous
Goldy's Restaurant on Broadway. There they sat for two
hours over highballs, talking and settling the future. They
did not talk much about the past, and about that moment
in Paris neither said a word.

About certain aspects of the future, Teverson was a bit
ambiguous. "I'm involved in a queer piece of business, Dex.
It's a delicate and even dangerous business in many ways,
but it pays. It suits me. No, it's not alcohol. Nor dope nor
anything of that nature. It's as legitimate, let's say, as guar-
anteeing second mortgages on condemned buildings or
promoting public utility holding companies."

Ward raised an eyebrow. "Are the police—ah—aware
of it?"

"No," dryly. "It remains that kind of business in spite of
all. That's one reason why I want you in the clear. The less
you know, the clearer in case of trouble. I need you, and it
looks as if you need me. But you're not needed inside the
lines."

"You'll have to come clearer, Tev. We've been old pals,
but I've got to know what kind of money I'm earning."

A queer, faint light flickered momentarily in Teverson's
pupils. Recollection, perhaps, of that moment in Paris. He
said, "It's good money."

"Clean money?"

"Absolutely. A hard job, but a clear one. I want you for
my bodyguard."

A world of comprehension began to dawn. "I see." Ward
paused. "I don't like it."

"If you saw a professional killer making a pass at me on Broadway tonight, Dex, what would you have done?"

Ward hesitated only a fraction of a second. "Thrown the Paramount Building at him."

"Why not take on the trick permanently? It's worth more, but I'll call it a hundred a week. I get around town a good bit. I don't want a mug along. I don't like their company socially. I don't trust them—for reasons. I'll use them only when I'm among their kind. You've always been a damned good shot, a dangerous fighter, you think quickly, and I know all there is to know about your nerve."

Ward shot him a look, seeking that light flickering in the dark pupils. "Tev," he said dryly, "there are plenty of professionals, trained to the job, who have all that and more."

"I don't want a professional." Teverson knocked the ash from his cigar, stared a moment at the glowing tip. He said, "I want a friend, Dex. I need a friend."

And Dex Ward sat there staring at him, silent. A friend! He thought at length, and yet he knew there could only be one answer.

2

THE HEEL

IT WAS A queer, glittering life, but Dex Ward found it a good life. It beguiled a man, thrilled him a bit, lulled the occasional doubt. Teverson maintained an enormous suite at the Hotel Blassingame under an assumed name. Ward had clothes, money, his own quarters. In addition to the hotel servants, who were well paid to keep their tongues, they had Ali, a tall, gaunt, silent Arab whom Teverson had picked up in Marseilles, to look to their comfort. The place at times swarmed with people, at intervals was deserted for days. All kinds of people came, glib Broadwayites and adventuresome debutantes in noisy droves, or parties of intent, rather furtive foreign men, excessively polite and formal, on carefully timed appointments and highly confidential business.

There was never, for Dex Ward, a least hint of the nature of this business. There was merely an undercurrent of tension, constantly. Ward often retired to his rooms, by tacit understanding, until the mysterious visitors were gone. Teverson often went abroad in the company of women, beautiful, jeweled women, but rarely did one remain alone. Of these the most frequent was Madame Gorda, Stephanie Gorda, young, darkly lovely, disturbing, and a mystery to

Ward. He could never figure out her relation to Teverson, whether intimacy, business, or mere friendship. Teverson was a strange man; he had taken women always in his stride, lightly, and he had never given himself heart and soul to any woman, nor, Ward thought, would he ever.

"He is a difficult man, this Teverson," she once remarked to Ward, smiling. This was persiflage, yet somehow significant; they were barely acquainted, speaking rarely, and then in a crowd. "He is so cold, so hard. He is too cold and hard. It is not real."

"You think so? Don't count on that."

"I *know*. If he were truly a cold, hard man I know what he would do, and he does not do it."

"Meaning exactly what?"

She laughed, with malice in her lovely eyes. But Ward was not to know the answer, for a pair of the ubiquitous foreign gentlemen bowed and claimed her attention.

It was a strange world indeed in which to be carrying for instant use, watchful and ready and none too certain, a powerful army .45 automatic and a merciless little Luger .25. A glittering world, but an uneasy one.

Sometimes, when Ward and Teverson dined alone together, a feeling of the old days came back. Teverson was fascinated by Ward's accounts of the lean years. They talked, ignoring the constant tension for an hour. Sometimes Teverson, in brooding mood, sat at the piano and began to play, passionately, wholly absorbed. Grieg and Rimsky-Korsakov and Liszt—music rhapsodizing the intoxication and the tragedy of life. They argued, heatedly, shouting at times, about the arts or philosophies or life,

damning each other for benighted imbeciles, then laughing it off over a double brandy.

And Dex Ward remembered that phrase—a friend!
And he let all doubts ride, and the automatics remained
untouched—oiled and ready and deadly, but so far unre-
quired.

Then came an evening when Ward was having a solitary
dinner at the apartment. Teverson had gone off on some
unstated business, leaving Ward to wait alone. He came
tearing in suddenly, tense and urgent.

"Finish that meal later," he commanded. "I've got to go
downtown. I want you along. Get your hat and coat on."

Philosophically Ward abandoned his second succulent
lamb chop and went along. They rode in a taxicab; Teverson
would own no private car that could easily be recognized.
He made no explanation, but gave an address far downtown on the West Side. It was on Calvert Street, just off the
waterfront, a seafaring neighborhood and an unsavory one.

The cab halted finally in a dark, narrow street. Teverson
first reconnoitered. A little ahead lay a seaman's outfitting
shop, a dingy cheap hotel, a tavern. The only person in
sight was a thin, vaguely pretty young girl in dingy finery
lounging in a glow of yellow gaslight in a nearby doorway. As the taxi drew up she came a little alert and began
to apply fresh make-up with an air of hopeful invitation,
glancing at the cab.

"All right, I guess," snapped Teverson. "Let's go."

THEY WALKED DOWN the street, past the girl and the
shop, and entered the tavern. Ward felt a tingling sensation of drama, a quickening of all alertness. For so quiet a
neighborhood the place was well patronized. Several noisy

card games proceeded at side tables, and the bar was lined with men. Two bartenders worked hard, while at the end of the bar a short, powerfully built man with small, sparkling blue eyes and ruddy cheeks idled with a proprietary air.

Teverson walked straight to the rear, nodding to the latter. The man nodded in return, expressionless. Teverson led the way through a door and along a passage to another room. Here were two round tables covered with green baize and a great many chairs and a blue haze of cigar smoke in which half a dozen men lounged, obviously waiting. They were a mixed lot, a hard lot, an interesting lot. They looked like ship's officers, tramp ships, quiet men, used to violence and danger.

Teverson looked over the gathering quickly, gave them terse greeting, and said curtly to Ward, "This'll do, Dex. Wait for me outside, please."

Ward's eyes narrowed a little. "I'll stay, if it's all the same."

"It isn't."

Ward shrugged and went out to the bar. He ordered a drink and studied the crowd through the bar mirror. He felt uneasy.

One of the card games broke up as he watched. The players, all young, swarthy men of dapper dress and soft, half snarling speech, were distinctly not seafaring men. They stretched, yawned, gossiped a bit, drifted off one by one. No one paid them any attention.

Ward considered striking up an acquaintance with the proprietor, but the latter defeated the idea by making leisurely departure to the rear. Ward swore to himself, ordered another drink, and then spent some time gingerly rebuffing the advances of a tottering huge fellow in a sheepskin jacket who swore he could lick any man in the house and desired Ward to select the man, any man. Any *two* men!

Presently Teverson and the proprietor returned. Teverson was in high good humor and paused for a drink. He introduced Ward.

"Meet an old friend, Dex. Duff Garry. An old importer friend."

Garry chuckled and shook hands.

Teverson went on, "He used to peddle the only Scotch in town you could trust."

"The old days is gone, Tev," said Garry. "Repeal is the blight of the land. Now if I was you I'd hurry along, not to change the subject. You can still trust me—and there were some strangers here, I'd not care to say the same for, who've taken themselves off since you came."

Teverson's smiling eyes looked frosty. "Thanks, Duff." He tossed off the drink, nodded to Ward. They took leave of the genial Garry.

Ward elbowed the tottering huge man out of the way at the door without ceremony and stepped ahead of Teverson into the street. The big fellow swore in indignation and violent gratification, reeled against the door, and unexpectedly hurled his mighty frame at the nearest figure, Teverson's.

Ward, whirling to break the drunken charge, spied from the corner of his eye a slender, furtive figure in the shadow of a dark doorway adjoining. He forgot the tottering berserk drunk. Something glinted evilly in the shadows, and then there was spurting flame and a thunder.

WARD INSTANTLY DROPPED the furtive killer with one

shot from the automatic. A frantic, bloodthirsty yell came from the other side of the doorway. A second gunman stood outlined in the light from the outfitting shop. A third came running from a doorway further up the street. He came firing.

The bark of the guns was paralyzing to the brain. Ward acted faster than thought could function, faster than deliberate volition could guide his purpose or his aim. A window of the tavern shivered and burst. Within was a pandemonium of terror.

Then abruptly there was a silence.

Ward saw three figures on the sidewalk, one perfectly still, two groveling in crippled anguish. Remotely up the street a fourth man ran madly, disappeared. There were no more. Ward turned to Teverson.

Teverson was down, sprawled over the threshold. Pinning him down was the huge fellow in the sheepskin. The big fellow lay still, a dead weight atop Teverson. Peculiarly still. There were four or five small unimpressive holes torn in the tough dun outer cloth of the jacket, squarely in the broad of his massive back. They had not been there a moment before.

Ward heaved the great figure from atop Teverson, rolled it aside. The man was palpably dead. Teverson lay there, breathing with difficulty. Ward looked him over, gripped him.

"Where'd they connect, Tev? Can you talk?"

Teverson swore viciously. "Drunken fool! My breath. Knocked breath clean out of me."

Ward felt, along with a small, quick agony of relief, a passing feeling of chill at that callous reaction to the death of a man. The drunk had taken the bullets. He had saved Teverson's life.

Then Duff Garry was with them, a burning fury of a man. "Man! That was close! The dirty bum! They've been hanging around for days. But I'll fix it. You get going. I'll say the drunk picked a fight, and they lay for him. But the drunk had a pal who shot them down and then ran for it. Get going, man!"

The taxi driver was still on hand, still half stunned by fright. They were in the cab before he could protest, and he fled with them away from there.

And that was how Dex Ward, ex-architect, ex-man of wealth, learned the exact nature of his job, and the use for which those automatics were designed and manufactured and hung upon his person. He was grim and silent as they sped home. He had never before killed a man.

The comfort and security of home rather failed to click tonight, even when Ali, sensing the need of the moment, brought a tray of drinks without waiting for orders. Teverson, after a curt, reassuring telephone conversation with Duff Garry, perched on the arm of a chair and watched Ward over his glass.

"Dex, we'll let the thanks go. You know the words. I don't mind saying, nevertheless, that it was a beautiful job."

"Skip it, skip it!"

Teverson studied him. "Feeling tough, eh?"

"Tough enough. How should I feel? Poetic?"

Teverson swirled the ice in his glass. "I think this will be good for you, Dex. Regardless of the ultimate outcome. Something's happened to you. Something you'll never get over."

"Doubtless—if the cops figure it out."

"They won't. Duff Garry will see to that. But let me explain what I mean. It's this. When those boys turned on the heat tonight, you were fused and cast again in a new mold, all in an instant. You'll never get back to the other again. I know. You'd better know. Whatever you do or become, you might say, architect, outlaw or bum, that instant will be in everything you do."

WARD GAZED AT him, slightly baring set, hard teeth. "That instant, presumably, will enter into any new bridge or building—make it a church—that I might conceivably be commissioned to design?"

"Exactly so!"

Ward stared, flinty of eye.

Teverson went on, "I'll tell you I've said that. I think I can talk straighter to you now than I ever could before. You weren't a man. You were a case of extended adolescence. Don't get mad; I'm not hazing you. You were brought up with the world in your lap. You never wanted for money. You never had need of ambition, pugnacity, ruthlessness. You never had need to learn the use of such things. If you wanted something, it was given to you. If you fought, it was for some intangible symbol, or just for the sheer hell of it." Faintly, passion entered his voice. "Have you ever wanted something so badly that you'd go out and raise blue hell with the entire world to get it?"

"I've been through hunger—I've wanted *food!*"

"Why? Why didn't you go out and get it? Why didn't you go fight tooth and nail and make the world deliver?"

Ward's jaw was set, silent.

"Simple!" Teverson said. "Because you were never the

man for it!" Ward stood up. He was red, then pale. Resentment, the memory of a thousand moments of desperation, were a fury in him. He thought of that moment in Paris. He thought of tonight. Abruptly the glass crushed in his hand.

"I'm getting out of here!"

"Oh, no, you're not."

"Why not?"

"Because I'm not going to allow you."

And then Ward saw the .25 automatic in Teverson's hand. Teverson's own weapon.

Teverson said, "You're still the adolescent. You want a run-out powder. You won't stay and take it."

"I took it tonight!"

"Because it came up and hit you in the face. You had no choice. Would you have shot those punks in cold blood?"

Ward was silent. Teverson snapped, "Even if you knew they were about to kill me? Or yourself?" Still no reply.

Teverson grunted. He placed the little automatic on a table. He deliberately stepped away from it and faced Ward.

"Now if you're so anxious to go, get started. But I'm going to shoot you down. You know I'll do it. You're pretty damned good on the draw. Possibly you can get me first. Make up your mind."

The silence was a palpable, tense thing, like steel about to snap with strain.

Ward came nearer. "What in hell are you trying to do to me? Break me? You know I'm not yellow. You know I'm out on a limb and the jitters are on me. I hit you once, but I've outgrown that. And I can't shoot you—not deliberately! Because I'd get you, Tev. By Judas, I'd get you!"

TEVERSON MET HIS gaze for a long moment. His face was a mask. Then one corner of his mouth twisted and he began to smile. He took out a cigarette and lighted it.

"You know, Dex," he drawled, "it's just barely possible that you're the only man in the world I couldn't shoot myself. I'd hate like hell to have to find out."

"You damned near did! It'd be the last thing you ever learned."

"I know, I know." Teverson dropped the pistol in his pocket. "Let's take your original suggestion. Skip it. It's a closed book. Pour another drink and sit down. I have an important phone call coming, and we'll have to wait around."

Ward stood staring at him a moment. Then he poured the drink. It was beyond him to figure it all out tonight.

In the first light of morning Ward was up and out for newspapers. He bought four of them, and over a steaming cup of coffee in an all night lunch room searched their columns. There was no mention of the gunbattle. He decided that these were early editions, and went back to the hotel and waited. About nine o'clock he bought four more. Still no mention. Not, in fact, till the early afternoon editions appeared did he find the story. And then it was a mere stick or two on an inside page:

TWO DEAD IN WATERFRONT BRAWL
Flying Bullets Terrify Neighborhood
Wounded Pair Give Incoherent Story

The story was vague, stereotyped.

Sidewalk battle preceded by altercation in saloon. Witnesses describe ambush. Score or more of shots. Police seeking unharmed survivors, believed in hiding. Two wounded in hospital protest they were "innocent bystanders," identified as petty criminals. Renewal of struggle for power among dock workers suspected.

In this muddled account the hand of Duff Garry was plain to be seen.

Ward had that evening to himself. Teverson, following several mysterious long distance conversations with Baltimore, suddenly decided to charter a plane and fly down there, risking it alone. Ward had a solitary dinner at Goldy's, then walked down Broadway. He paused moodily to watch the performance of his successor in uniform before the burlesque house, suddenly came to a decision, and halted a cab. He rode down to the lower West Side and got out two blocks from Duff Garry's, continuing afoot. He was watchful, wary.

From the corner, Ward examined the scene of the battle the night before. The street looked exactly as he first saw it, a furtive, lonely looking street with a thousand secrets behind its sordid outer aspect. Even the girl in the gaslit doorway was here again tonight. Ward strolled along the sidewalk.

The girl watched him. Ward looked at her. She smiled, vainly, nervously. She was blond, thin, pathetic, hardly more than a child. Ward paused, leaned on the stoop railing.

"How's it, sister? All alone?"

She giggled, gave him a bold look. "I am, but I don't like it much."

"How about dating a guy then?"

"It's a cinch."

"Fine. Where can we get a drink?" It seemed as if her breath caught a little. "I've got a drink. Why spend your money at a bar?"

"You pour me a drink and I'll pay you for it. I've got enough of what it takes."

She smiled, patted straw-colored puffs of hair. "O.K. Let's go upstairs."

IT WAS A squalid place: two tiny lonely rooms redolent of ancient cooking and old linoleum and sunless living. They sat at a small deal table beneath a Welsbach light. That white illumination revealed in the girl's blue eyes a look of deeply buried fear, a hunted look, that she strove to cover with an eager, entertaining smile.

Ward placed a five dollar bill on the table. "That's just a calling card, sister. There's more, if you'll help me out."

The smile turned uncertain.

"How?"

"I'm an awfully ignorant guy. There are a lot of things I want to learn. About this neighborhood and some of the people in it."

She turned pale, staring at him. "Are you a copper?"

He smiled firmly, shook his head. "If I were a detective I wouldn't be wasting my time sitting here talking to you, sister. We'd already be on our way to the Charles Street station house together. Look here. Do you know a man named Teverson?"

The blue eyes widened, and she shook her head vehemently. "No. I never heard of him."

He studied her. "Yes, you have. He was around here last night."

"He was?"

"And I was with him."

Recognition suddenly shot through her. She cowered in her chair a little.

Ward said, "I'm not going to harm you, baby. But I'd appreciate a bit of a line on what's been said along this block today. I'd like to know, for instance, if the folks really know who those boys were who started the shooting. You saw them yourself."

The girl, Ward knew, sat there exactly as she would sit if he held a gun trained on her across the table. She lived in a world of men, lived by their cruelty and their kindness, and her illusions, if any, were illusions of dread.

"I saw them," she said. "I didn't know them. I heard who they were, though. Nobody's talking if they can help it, but it got around. Those were some of the Eel gang."

"Eel?"

"Jules Koerner—The Eel. Don't you know who I mean?"

"Tell me more. This is very interesting."

She couldn't quite understand, but she obeyed. There was a fatalism in her, a submission to this man's cool, and possibly deadly, insistence. In her own simple terms she told an extraordinary story.

3

STEPHANIE

JULES KOERNER WAS a mysterious and sinister man of power who worked beyond the routine rackets of the big town. Since he offered them no competition, they left him alone. They'd have been hard put to find him, in any case, since he rarely was seen, even by his own men, who were directed by his few trusted lieutenants. His territory was the waterfront, the docks and shipping of the great harbor. His evil trade was unknown in its entirety.

The water rats, the petty thieves who furtively nibbled at the rich cargoes handled at the piers, lived in terror of him, and rendered willing tribute. The longshoremen, valiant and violent souls whose bloody wars were legendary, walked shy of trouble with The Eel.

The seamen who sailed into the harbor on the ships of every nation were well acquainted with his name, and if not, were warned to shut their eyes to any of The Eel's business they might see. Many, it was rumored, were in his employ. There were hints of smuggling, of narcotics, of wholesale illegal entry of Asiatics.

"I've heard so many things about The Eel," the girl said. "I don't know how much is truth or made up. There's so much goes on. It's always gone on, but never before like this, with one man running everything, nobody ever seeing him, everybody afraid to do anything that might get them in wrong. Do you know how many bodies the police have picked up in the water the past year?"

"How many?"

"One a day. That's average. Some days there's more than one. Nobody knows how they got there, but they find them. The police will tell you that."

"Victims of The Eel?"

She shivered, and glanced around her involuntarily. "That ain't for me to say. I've… I've talked too much already. I've told you all that I know."

"Well, let's change the subject. What's known around here about Teverson? About his racket?"

She shook her head, shrugged a little. "Honest, I couldn't tell you a thing about him. I only heard the name a couple of times. All I know is The Eel has the mark on him, and some way they're enemies."

Ward knew she spoke the truth. He frowned. He was getting somewhere, but certainly at a snail's pace. He got up.

"Sister, you'll keep your ears open, won't you? I may be back again. Just for friendship's sake, I'll leave this with you, too." He peeled three additional five dollar bills from a roll and dropped them on the table.

She looked at the money, at Ward, and there was disbelief and gratitude in her eyes. He poured a short drink, lit a cigarette, and she watched him. Then in a small, curious voice, the voice both of a dubious child and of a wistful age-long wisdom, she said, "Do you like me a little bit?"

He grinned, tilted her chin. "I think you're swell. Sometime we'll have a party together."

"Will we?" eagerly. The blue eyes gazed intently. "You know… you're different."

"Not much, sister."

She smiled a little tolerant smile; she knew better. She followed him to the door. She plucked his sleeve just a little, leaned against the wall. She looked tired and content, watching him.

He grinned, winked, and closed the door and walked down the gloomy, almost fetid hall.

A sudden sound of running halted him at the top of the stairs. Someone mounting steps hurriedly. It came from above, with a furtive note in the very sound. Then it ceased.

He waited. There was a feeling in this place. It was like a tomb, quiet, with the sound of the living coming only through the shadowed walls. Yet he knew he was not alone. He felt, by a sixth sense, eyes fixed steadily on him, baleful eyes staring in malignancy and hatred.

In a moment he descended the stairs. He walked without attempt at concealment. Two flights through gloom. In the entrance corridor he moved swiftly, gaining the door, opening it, letting it swing shut while he retreated noiselessly into the dark recess far at the rear. There, invisible, he took a stand, watching.

Above, someone suddenly came rushing down the stairs. The old stair casing trembled with the plunging descent. It was a man, a powerful, tall figure in the obscurity. He rushed the door, paused, then opened the door unhurriedly and strolled outside.

WARD WATCHED HIM through the frosted glass. The man

stood in the outer doorway, just in off the stoop. He peered one way and then another. The set of his shoulders hinted at indecision, aggravation. Ward smiled dryly and walked to the door.

The man merely turned his head as Ward walked out. The face was lantern-jawed, scarred, challenging. And in the gaslight Ward saw something flicker over jet pupils that was like a cloud passing over the sun.

Ward said, "Got a match, friend?"

The man grunted. For a second he did not move; then he produced a book of matches. Ward offered a cigarette. The man took one, almost fumbling it.

Ward touched the flame to his own cigarette, then held out the light to the man. The radiance from his cupped hands shone full on the sinister features of that face. The scar had split the right eyebrow, creased the length of the nose. Abruptly, as if just realizing, the jet eyes rolled, glancing at Ward; instantly, with a breath, the man blew out the flame.

"Thanks," said Ward, returning the matches. He smiled grimly. "Do the same for you sometime."

The man breathed a single foul expletive. It was meaningless, only half audible, involuntary. Ward stepped to the sidewalk and began to walk to the corner, away from the direction of Duff Garry's.

He had taken not twenty steps when he broke into a run. Behind him sounded a whistle, a peculiar shrill signal. Ward left the sidewalk and ran in the middle of the asphalt paving. He was nearing the corner.

From concealment at each corner, two men appeared, stepping out into the street to meet him. Ward did not pause, but increased speed. The men brandished no guns, but things swung from their hands, loose, weighted objects likely to be lengths of rubber hose loaded with shot.

Closing in on the grim, avid pair, Ward unexpectedly threw himself into a plunging dive. He caught them unawares. The man he tackled was catapulted off his feet, head over heels, and his skull cracked resoundingly on the pavement. Ward rolled sidewise. The second man charged him.

Ward lay on his back, knees bent, feet off the ground, looking at the fellow. The rubber hose flailed at him; Ward parried the blow with one quick foot. The thug closed in, swinging the punishing loaded hose. Ward fended the thing with his hands, hooked one foot behind the other's left heel and kicked the man's left knee sharply. There was a sharp splintering and a scream. The man collapsed with a shattered knee.

Ward got up with a sudden spring, gripping the automatic butt inside his coat. There was a man on the sidewalk, the man of the gas-lit doorway. The fellow stood in frozen indecision, his own hand in a side coat pocket, staring at Ward, staring at the two broken men stretched out on the paving.

Ward relaxed, smiled grimly. The gunman dared not fire and attract police, not while his comrades lay there helpless to escape. And he dared not attack Ward—not with such evidence before him.

Ward drawled, "Come pick up your marbles, pal. The game is over."

He turned and walked away rapidly. He was not

followed. He was a long time returning home, making certain of that.

WARD PONDERED ON this adventure, and came to certain fixed conclusions. First, that he would not tell Teverson about the affair. Second, that he was definitely not being trailed; the gang was naturally watching the neighborhood closely, and had observed his arrival. Third, that it was probably their usual method to avoid unnecessary shooting, with its attendant embarrassments, and rather to slug a victim by stealth and spirit him to the piers and drop him into the swirling running tides of the Hudson River. There was a shudder in the thought. Indirectly, it caused him to think again of that queer, inexplicable feeling in the tenement hallway—that sensation of malignant eyes staring, boring into him.

He pondered other things. The Eel! He remembered once, years ago as a boy, sitting on a stringpiece of a pier on the Hudson looking down at the restless black waters. A thing swam into sight, a long black evil thing, weaving in and out of the piles, sinuous and sinister. Later he knew it to be simply a water creature, but to his young imagination it was a monster and terrifying.

If Teverson were an enemy of The Eel, then he must be a rival. And as a rival, must compete with The Eel on his own grounds. It seemed logical, and yet… yet, for all the ruthlessness of the man, Ward could not believe it of Teverson. The thought was monstrous.

And then he remembered again that episode in Paris.

Teverson had flown back in the night and was in the apartment when Ward awakened. They ate breakfast together. Teverson, glancing over the morning paper, made a sound and bent absorbedly over some news story.

"More excitement on Duff Garry's block," he murmured.

Ward came alert, wary. "What now?"

"Girl..." Teverson paused. "Now I wonder! Could it be that kid we saw?"

Ward snatched the paper.

POLICE SUSPECT MURDER
IN GIRL'S GAS DEATH

The theory of suicide first accepted when police broke down the door of a bleak tenement flat at 17 Calvert Street late last night and found the pathetic dead body of Jessie Wilson, 19, lying on a disheveled bed in gas-filled rooms, was exploded by the report of the Medical Examiner, who rushed the autopsy at the request of the Homicide Squad. No evidence of gas poisoning was found in the organs of the dead girl, who was said to be in perfect health at the time of her death. Money was found in her purse; no motive for suicide could be established. It is now suspected that the girl was brutally murdered.

Deputy Chief Inspector Firkin stated that the investigation will pursue the theory that the killer first suffocated the girl in her bed with a pillow and then turned on the gas to cover up the crime. The police claim to have found valuable clues.

The girl was pretty and lived alone. She was well known in the neighborhood, but had no known enemies. The mystery may take an added importance because of the two unsolved killings in the shooting affray a few doors away the night before.

Ward read it over twice. All the incredulity of the living in the face of death was in him; realization was like sluggish gears starting, turning, gaining slow momentum. Jessie Wilson! He had not even known her name. Suffocated! He thought of her bold childish desperation, the pathos of her eager, entertaining smile. He thought of his own unwitting responsibility for this. The gears whined into speed, and there was a murderous fury in Dex Ward. He stood up suddenly.

Teverson said, "What the hell's the matter with you?"

Ward looked at him. His face set, and he battled within himself. "The creeping vermin! Why didn't I throttle the three of them?"

"Three of what?"

"Listen to me, Tev! Are you in the same racket? Are you following the same lines as that gang?"

TEVERSON WIPED HIS mouth carefully with the napkin. He was sober, wary. "I don't know what you're talking about, Dex. Explain from the beginning and maybe I can give you an answer."

Ward knew he was talking too much. He paced away from the table, across the room and back. His mind worked clearly again. "Look here. That girl saw the shooting. The fellow who got away ran right past her. She could identify him."

"Yes," said Tev. But his gaze was intense, piercing. "And what about throttling the three of them?"

"Certainly the three! The two wounded and the one that got away. They're alive, aren't they?"

Teverson nodded. Ward watched his face. He seemed to accept the explanation. Ward felt grim relief; he was not yet ready to disclose his part in the tragedy. That outburst had almost done it for him.

Teverson said, "It clicks. And it's like them."

"Who?"

"Some bad friends I have. And— oh, yes! You asked if I was in the same racket. What racket?"

"Killing women will do. If they're bad friends, they must have a reason."

Teverson, seated deep in his chair, brooded a while. He was slow to approach his reply. "Dex, they have an excellent reason. But I'm not in their racket. I'm not that bad. I don't have to be… And I'm not ready even yet to tell you all my business, and I'm sorry."

"Sorry, hell!" snorted Ward impatiently. "Why all the mystery now? I'm in deep enough, certainly!"

Teverson smiled wryly. He pulled a wad of bills from his pocket and peeled off ten one-hundred dollar bills. "I suppose it was a mistake, Dex. There's ten weeks' salary. There'll be no hard feelings."

"Are you firing me?"

"No, I'm simply giving you your powder."

Ward was savagely impelled to knock him clear across the room with one blow. "I asked if I were being fired, Ted!"

"You're not."

"Then I'm staying."

"That's fine." Teverson studied him. "But why the high fever? What's got into you? Ideals? Women have been murdered before."

Ward walked back to his chair and sat down. "I don't know. When you've been down yourself… and you see somebody else who's down, away down, and who gets stepped on like a miserable worm by some dirty, motherless, murdering thug—dammit, Tev, I'm only human! I saw the kid the other night myself. It's under my skin."

"I understand. Only not too deep, Dex! Things that get under too deep require a sharp knife to remove them. Forget it. There's nothing we can do about it now." Ward agreed.

Nevertheless, it was with a queer confusion of emotion that Ward unexpectedly came upon Teverson telephoning later in the day. Teverson did not see him in the doorway. Teverson was talking to a certain "Skipper." The "Skipper" was one of the biggest gamblers on Broadway, a man of money and friends and influence.

"Give her the works, Skip. I don't want my hand in it, but I'll settle the bill with you. Nothing too fancy, but as decent a layout as possible. Find a plot for her and dig up a parson and see she gets a proper funeral. No, I'm neither the long lost husband nor have I turned sap all of a sudden. I have my reasons. I feel like giving the kid the only break she ever got. Okay! G'by!"

WARD RETREATED SILENTLY, unobserved, to try in deep puzzlement to figure that one out.

The events of the past few days presaged an imminence of crisis in the affairs of Teverson. Ward could feel it. Teverson was on edge. The glib Broadwayites were missing now, and there were many urgent telephone conversations and furtive messages and even cablegrams over which Teverson spent long periods, decoding the garbled words.

Ward roamed restively, but he bided his time. He was needed, and he stood by his bargain.

Several times they rushed off without warning on emergency errands, once to a great Fifth Avenue jewelers, again to the Customs House, another time to a rendezvous deep in Central Park, where a stranger was picked up and Ward dropped and told to wait, and where an hour later the exchange was reversed again, all without explanation. Ward felt, sensed, somewhere beyond these inscrutable maneuvers an outer field of action, a front line where violence ruled and death was stalking.

He bided his time. He did a job, as contracted, but he bided his time. He brooded, thinking of a head of straw-colored hair in yellow gaslight and of an eager, entertaining smile. He thought of a face with an ugly scar. There was no romantic notion in him; there was pity, pity that desired passionately to be transmitted into action. He waited.

One evening soon Teverson entertained a visitor alone. It was Stephanie Gorda. Ward retired to his own rooms shortly after her arrival, wondering again about the woman. The furtive foreign men who called addressed her always with intense respect as "Madame Gorda." Teverson called her "Stephanie." She wanted something, wanted it with persistence and determination, and Ward could see that in her eyes, for all their veiled, adroit bedazzlement of every man who came within their range.

Stephanie Gorda was an unusual type, difficult to define, difficult to place in point of origin. She was young, not more than twenty-one, yet she possessed the fascinating maturity of a world-traveled woman of thirty. She was tall, dark, with a lovely youthful figure, exquisitely groomed. She was extensively informed, and she could talk absorbingly, with a quaint touch of unfamiliar accent, with any man. She was a beautiful woman, and she knew it.

Ward watched her whenever she was in the same room; she became a disturbing symbol, in a way, of a world he once had known and lost.

Late in the evening Teverson came into Ward's room.

His dark eyes flashed sparks and there was a kind of angry exasperation in him.

"I've got a job for you, Dex. I'll be busy. I want you to escort Stephanie home."

"Job?" dryly. "That's a pleasure."

"Perhaps," Teverson snapped. "It's still a job, and you're to work at it."

Ward eyed him, speculating. It looked like a rift in the relation, whatever its nature. "Go on."

"She'll show you where she lives. It's a bit out of the way. You go right along. But come right back. Keep your eyes wide open—both for trouble you might meet and trouble right on your hands."

"What kind?"

"She has some bad friends herself. And also, she'll very likely be highly inquisitive. Keep your mouth closed, do a job, and get back here."

4

HIDE-AWAY

THEY DEPARTED IN a cab from the hotel line. The girl gave a Brooklyn address which the driver did not know. She directed him to cross the Brooklyn Bridge and take further directions later. Ward frowned as they set out; that address sounded to him like a Red Hook neighborhood. The waterfront again!

Stephanie talked, casually, unimportantly. For a time. Then the questions began; inevitably, Ward concluded.

"You know Mr. Teverson long, Mr. Ward?"

"A while."

"You are friends? But he employs you, of course!"

"We're friends, and I work for him. A little of both."

"You are, shall I say, his confidant?"

"Naturally."

"You are not very loquacious, Mr. Ward."

"Not very," he agreed.

She laughed a little, took a cigarette from her bag. "It is so that you entertain your American girls when you are with them?"

"I don't entertain them."

"They entertain you?"

"Neither. I leave them alone." He struck a match and

held it for her cigarette, and she gazed at him over the flame. Her eyes were luminous in the tiny light, studying him. The perfume of her, subtle and rare, was in his nostrils, and he was aware of the closeness of her with all his being.

"I know," she said suddenly. "You are, what you call, a woman hater!"

She made a quick face at him. She simply flashed clean under his guard. He laughed, explosively. "Oh, no! Simply broke, busy, and not sufficiently bothered at the moment by any special woman. I'll get around to that in time."

"That is better," she approved. "Now I like you."

"That's fine. I like you. Under other circumstances I'd want terribly to come around with a box of gardenias under my arm and take you out and show you the town."

"I should like very much to see New York. With you."

He looked at her. "See New York? It's all around you."

"But I mean what you mean. The New York that you know well. I do not see this town."

"Why not?"

She shrugged. "There are reasons why I must not show myself too much. Where I go, I go hurrying, hiding as much as possible. I have much to do."

Ward swore inwardly. More mystery! He declined to exhibit any curiosity. "That's too bad," he said calmly. He reminded himself dryly of Teverson's warning.

The cab came to a pause for lights; they were driving south on lower Manhattan's main highway, Lafayette Street. The girl puffed on the cigarette, leaned to the window to toss it outside. And without warning she hurled herself back in the seat. She cringed against Ward with a low cry of terror.

Instinctively his hand gripped the automatic. "What's wrong?"

"Look! There! In that car."

Across the intersection a lone car waited, northbound. It was a big powerful black sedan, and two men occupied it. They were large men, dark of complexion, mustached. The burning gaze of both was fixed on the taxicab.

THE MEN EXCHANGED a word, and the man beside the driver opened the door quickly and got out.

Stephanie cried, "Go, driver! Quickly! Go away from here!"

Ward tapped on the glass with his gun. "Get going, stupid!" he barked. "You hear the lady?"

"The lights," said the driver. "They're still red."

"Get going!" Ward roared.

They got going.

Stephanie clung to Ward, a little hysterical. "They've found me! What shall I ever do now? They have been looking for me for so long."

"Who are they? What will they do to you?" Ward was looking through the rear window, watching the big car make an abrupt swinging turn in the avenue.

"They would kill me. They are my countrymen."

Ward swore, yelled to the driver. "Put your foot to the floor, mug! Your life is in this. Lose that car!"

"I'll find a cop," called the frightened driver. "A cop somewhere."

"No police!" Stephanie protested. "Please, no police!"

Ward moved forward, leaned out beside the driver, exhibited the automatic. "You'll keep going, you hear?

Three blocks below, turn left, turn east. Stick to the narrow streets. Give her all she's got."

"Okay—okay!" the driver stuttered. He sent the sturdy taxicab roaring down the almost empty thoroughfare between darkened factories and deserted office buildings.

The big car was after them, gaining on them. Their lead was a good one, but never could they lose that car late at night on any broad uncrowded avenue. Ward was silent; he held Stephanie in his arms firmly, ready. Suddenly the cab made a screaming swoop into a narrow ancient street leading eastward, a street of tenements and occasional parked cars, scattered sidewalk groups. The horn blasted away before them.

"Stephanie," said Ward. "You've got to jump."

"Jump? They will see me. They will run me down."

"I'll fix that."

"But you?"

"I'll lead them a chase," he said grimly. "I'll get them clear!"

Ward again addressed the driver. "Get this, you! Don't miss it. Make east for the river. The market streets. The pavings are still wet from the night's flushing. You know how to make a skidding stop, reversing direction?"

The driver agreed.

Ward said, "Cut a corner. Swing her sharp, and stop her dead, close to the curb. I'll jump into the street. The woman out the other side. She'll make for the shadow of a market shed and hide. I'll give them all I've got in both my guns and start running. You beat it—fast, any direction. They'll follow one or the other, and it doesn't matter which, so long as they miss her."

"Oh," moaned Stephanie, "but they can stop also! They will hunt you down."

"They're damned well doing a good job of it right now! I want a fighting chance."

She prayed, "Must this be always?"

From behind came a staccato sound, as of drumming, muffled by the engine's roar.

WARD COMMANDED THE maneuver. The driver was an automaton. They flew past sidewalks where late strollers, wise in the ways of the city, screamed and dived for shelter from gunfire. They missed cross traffic by miracles. They passed into a gloomy, utterly deserted neighborhood where huge gaunt buildings loomed. Truck platforms and sheds hid each sidewalk in dank shadow. The very air smelled of wet asphalt and fresh produce, and the pavements wore a sheen of light.

"Turn here!" Ward snapped.

The driver cut the wheel. He was an expert. The city, the world, spun madly. The cab twice slithered completely about. The driver worked the wheel in a frenzy. The cab slowed, ceased gyrating; the wheels bumped sidewise against the curb. They were motionless.

Ward kicked open the sidewalk door, shoved Stephanie through it. "Under cover! Quick!"

He burst through the opposite door, ran back toward the corner. He drew both guns. Roaring to crescendo, the big car hit the crossing like a blazing meteor; the tires shrieked with the turn. The driver spied the halted cab, jammed on the brakes, and tried to halt the vast momentum of the black car.

Ward, standing full in the light from the corner lamp

post, roared defiance to attract their attention, and immediately opened fire, planting his bullets quickly, carefully.

The effect was instantaneous. Before his eyes occurred the uttermost miracle. The big car was lurching on the wet pavement, unable to stop on the instant. Instead of persisting, halting and returning, the driver stepped on the gas! The wheels now spun desperately, seeking traction. The rubber caught, and like a bolt the big car disappeared around the next corner in full mad flight.

Ward stood fixed to the spot. The abrupt silence was a sudden pressure on the ears. It took a space of time for instinct to resign, reason to return.

Stephanie came running, limping slightly. "You're not hurt? Oh, you're not hurt?"

"I'm all right. What on earth happened?"

"The police. They ran away."

"Police? I haven't seen any. Not yet!"

"*You* were the police!" She laughed, still a little in the grip of hysteria. "Oh, don't you see? You stood in the light and you yelled so loudly at them. They were but speeding by, they did not see you so good. Who but a policeman and a very brave one would command them as if to halt? They fled, they do not want the police either!"

Ward shook his head.

Just then the taxi driver tottered from his cab. Immediately his knees buckled and he collapsed to the pavement.

Ward ran to him. "Steady, boy! I'm sorry!"

"Sorry, hell! I ain't hurt."

Ward got him to his feet, and he went on, "My legs is too wobbly to stand. Don't *ever* do that to me again!"

Ward laughed. His lungs filled, his body filled. "You sit

on the floor. I'll drive her for you. And in a hurry. The race will start a general alarm all over the East Side."

He remembered something, and turned to Stephanie. "Damn, I forgot! Are you all right, Stephanie?"

"My ankle pains a very little," she said, smiling. "Otherwise nothing."

"Then we'll get going."

THEY DROVE SLOWLY, sedately now. There was no interference. Their taut nerves eased. They gained the bridge without mishap, and crossed the magnificent old span, high above the city where the heavens are reversed and a myriad lights twinkle in darkness below. There was no talk.

Stephanie directed Ward, once they were in Brooklyn. They drove down to the ancient piers, where India men once unloaded, their lofty masts and yards rocking gently with the tides. Not a soul was in sight. The cab halted in a kind of alley among the gloomy dock buildings. Ward looked around him, wary, uneasy. Stephanie reached quickly in her purse and rewarded the driver handsomely.

"You will please say nothing of this evening? It would perhaps be best."

"Lady, I've had narrow escapes!" said the man earnestly. "Don't you worry. Those guys won't find out who drove this cab through any of my talk!"

She waited till he was gone. Then she walked a little distance along a footpath in darkness between the huge wooden buildings. She knocked at a door, a distinctive signal. A wait, and a man's voice in a foreign tongue. She responded similarly, and the door opened quickly with a sliding of bolts.

Stephanie took Ward's hand. She led him through pitch

darkness, redolent of ancient, aromatic cargoes, conversing softly with the unseen man. They argued over something, but she turned imperious, and the man subsided. Not a word of this unknown tongue could Ward understand, other than the man's name, Carl, but he knew he was unwelcome here.

She told Ward, "We do not use a light. It is a good precaution."

"Where on earth are we going?"

"To where I am living. You will see."

Ward wondered rather grimly how far Teverson's warning was meant to apply. He heard the water lapping at the piles somewhere beneath them. Another door was opened, and he was cautioned to watch for the stairs. They passed below. And Ward's eyes, becoming accustomed to darkness, began to make out the dim light of the harbor night filtering through, and he was aware of the smell and nearness of harbor water. They were in a cavernous space under the pier.

Now the man made use of a light, a tiny pencil beam that barely indicated their path along a sort of crude platform over the water. They walked a short distance away from land, and Ward was astonished to discover a lean, fast looking water runabout rocking gently at the side of the platform. The tide was at the ebb, and the craft was quite a drop below. Stephanie sprang to the deck with the ease of familiarity. Ward followed.

Stephanie led him to the leather-cushioned cockpit at the stern. The man cast off, propelled the boat toward the pier's end by thrusting with a boathook. The boathook also served when they came to the palisade of solid timbers supporting the far end of the pier. He maneuvered with it—and a section of that wall of piles swung back on hinges. It was a false section in the bank of pilings. The boat eased itself through gently, the section was closed again, and they were adrift in the murmuring harbor tide.

THE MAN ALLOWED the boat to drift a little while before he started the engine. It snorted, there was a great churning, and then, like a hound, it found its course, baying, speeding, bouncing a little on the swell. The night breeze sang in their ears. Around them the water was slick with dancing reflected radiance, and the whole world was a world of twinkling distant lights, teeming, exciting, beckoning.

"You like this?" said Stephanie. "In my country we have nothing like this."

Ward, permitting himself to relax a little alongside her, could not resist the awesome strangeness and the beauty of it. "It's magnificent!"

"I am glad. You are my prisoner now, eh?"

He felt a sense of chill. "I am?"

"You do not like to be Stephanie's prisoner?"

"I can hardly say—yet!"

She laughed softly. "We shall see." They sped into the wind and the night, into darkness and magnificence and mystery.

Ward was prepared for almost anything, but he was a little puzzled when they turned into a dark mass of wharf and warehouse indistinguishable from their starting point. He had no idea where they were. The man at the tiller idled the engine, flashed the pencil beam of light once, twice, three times. From the gloom came a rapid answering flash. The boat moved in, straight for blank darkness.

They had to duck their heads to clear the low opening through which they passed. A man on an invisible landing guided the boat. Stephanie said, "I do not have this so well fixed because it does not matter so much as the other. The other is clever, you think? If I am pursued in a car, I take to water and they cannot follow. I have not been discovered here yet."

Ward grunted, having no argument. He stumbled after her in pitch darkness up a flight of stairs, along a passage, another stairs, and through a door into a lighted room. It was a small bright room, serene and clean and empty but for a chair and an absurdly matter of fact umbrella stand. Stephanie opened a further door, and he peered in on a severely and richly furnished living room. It was a luxurious apartment! All lacking was window openings.

In a moment Ward had several things figured out. They were well above the water line, perhaps a bit inshore, probably within the shell of a rickety abandoned warehouse. This apartment, concealed from the outer world was a perfect hide-out. The clear, fresh air, gently in motion, meant a system of artificial ventilation. The furnishings indicated taste and care—and much money.

5

PLANS FOR BERENGARIA

STEPHANIE MADE HIM comfortable on an enormous, deep cushioned piece of furniture fashioned in a wide, capacious semicircle. She placed a tray of bottles and glasses and ice on a table, and seated herself opposite him.

"Now! We talk."

He poured three fingers of Scotch.

"About what?"

"About you."

"That's out."

"About Mr. Teverson then."

"That's out also."

"Then we talk about me."

He smiled, eyes narrowed. "That's rather better." He waited. This, he suspected, was to be a battle of wits, and a bit grimly he welcomed it. He had objectives of his own.

She smoked her cigarette for a moment, and her mood changed. A deep and smoldering intensity manifested itself. She was a creature who shuttled back and forth in manner between the coquette of twenty and the firm woman of thirty at will, constant only in her disturbing beauty.

"I am an exile," she said. "I will talk frankly with you.

My country is in ruins, my father is in hiding. I am here in America to accomplish certain things for my father and my country, and I find great difficulty. You in America do not know what this is. But I, born at the beginning of the war, have lived all a lifetime in trouble and fighting and bloodshed. You must understand that to understand me and what it is I desire."

"I've been through most of postwar Europe," said Ward. "I can understand a little."

She told him her story in outline, speaking in a low tone of subdued passion. Her home was in the republic of Berengaria in southeastern Europe. The war and the Treaty of Versailles had left her country diminished in size, impoverished.

Her father, after distinguished service in the field, had perceived the futility of war, had championed a rather futile form of political pacifism, and with the war-weary millions of his countrymen behind him, had advanced through a stormy political career to the highest post in the land, that of Premier.

He was either too early or too late. The time was utterly wrong for his cause, his methods. Europe resounded with the tread of marching men. Dictators ruled. He fought with all his mind and heart to stem the tide in his own land, but it rolled over him, swept him from power. His Minister of War, ambitious and treacherous, had obtained the arms the country lacked from the warlike dictator of a neighboring nation, and his seizure of government was effected in a single, bloody movement upon the capital.

"He rules now," said Stephanie. "My father hides, far in the hills where the peasants guard him vigilantly. I left

Ward was taking no chances

him there, made escape and came to America. I have no
real passport, only a fake one for emergency, that is why
I do not go out too much or wish to have to do with the
police. A few of my exiled countrymen are here—they
keep my secret. If I accomplish what I plan, I can return.
If not. She shrugged.

"What's your plan?"

"Arms!" she declared. "To save my country. The War
Minister has sold out his people. How do you think he
procured his munitions? By agreeing to the surrender of
our liberties to another nation, to the dictator who rules
with iron hand to the north of us. They wait only the proper
time. It is soon here—and Berengaria is no more!"

"Are your people really anxious to take up arms against
them?"

"They beg for them! For a thousand years they have
been a free people, fierce and independent. They are help-

less now. But they gather in the hills, they drill and make ready, living in hope. They have studied the strategy of the Rebellion in Ireland. They have learned from the tactics of the War Minister himself. My father even—he is a soldier again, for he has seen that liberty is not only to be won, but must be held, even at the cost of life itself. He stays behind, to be ready; I am here, to make possible the day of rescue."

"Who were those fellows in the black car tonight?"

"Secret agents. I knew those two men. Too well. They are traitors, terrorists. They are here to find me. It is known I am here already. It is suspected why. Assassination is no new thing to them—they are skilled at it. They will look desperately for me now that they have once seen me."

"And what's holding you up?"

SHE WAS A little weary. "Everything. There is an embargo on arms. Not by this country; but over there. It is the usual thing. The big fellows say they are neutral and that no arms may go to either side. But when one side has arms and munition factories, it means only that they tie the hands of the little fellow who has none.

"We have no port to the sea. The countries surrounding do not permit shipments of guns to pass."

"Then how do you expect to get them in?"

"I do not know. I only hoped. I hoped that Teverson would find a way. He is so clever, so experienced."

Ward leaned forward, a bit on edge. "How do you figure that he can arrange for the arms and ammunition you want?"

"He has the means more than anybody I know. He has the organization of ships and sailors and agents and communications. For two years he has been building this up. He has helped many.

"It was through him that we first obtained funds after the *coup d'état* and the great land confiscations. Funds we must have.

"All the rich people of our party gave up their hidden jewels, their plate, their secret treasures. Not since the wars of the Middle Ages have people put their wealth into moveable treasure as in the past fifteen years. All the countries have forbidden to export a penny of wealth beyond the borders. And all the countries have political exiles, fugitives with a price on their heads.

"They who were once rich cannot reach their wealth. They would starve—if it were not for Teverson."

Ward turned that amazing statement over rapidly in his mind. It clicked!

It explained mysteries.

"Has he supplied you with the funds that you have now?"

"Every penny. I arrived in America by steerage. On a freighter. I was smuggled ashore by his own men. They also smuggled ashore, little by little, a great store of treasure. All that wealth and my life itself was in the hands of rough men, and not a penny lost, not an insult to me. He has power, that Teverson."

"Where have you got your funds now?"

"Some is in the bank. Oh, several banks. It is about half a million dollars. Some more I have in gold, hidden. It is the national treasury of Berengaria."

Ward studied her. Half a million! Frozen up cold. And those slender, lovely, and so very young hands controlled the treasury of a nation.

"What has Teverson had to say to your proposals, Stephanie?"

"He says—impossible! There is no seaport, he cannot operate. Jewels and treasure, yes. Guns and ammunition cannot be hidden, cannot be taken secretly across another country. He refuses to consider. And there is no one else." She leaned forward to pour a glass of ruby wine from a decanter. "Unless... you know someone, some way, Dex Ward."

"I?"

She gazed intensely over the rim of the little glass. "You are a confidant of Teverson. He refuses to discuss with me. All right, I will discuss with you. You know perhaps how this thing may be accomplished?"

Ward grunted. He got up, strolled across the room, swirling his highball. "Do you know anything of a person known hereabouts as 'The Eel,' Stephanie?"

She sat erect. "The Eel? Who is this? He is Teverson's enemy, no?"

"Correct."

"You mean... *he* might do this for me?"

"Not exactly. What do you know about him?"

"ONLY THAT BEFORE I have this place prepared to hide in, I am watched for many days by strange men. They are not my countrymen and they did no harm while I remained at the little hotel. They seem not sure, not decided about me. Once only did one speak to me. He approached quietly and asked if I were not from Berengaria, and he tried to discuss a business proposition. A more favorable proposition, he said, than I had. I saw he was ignorant; that he was, you say, fishing. I hurried to tell Teverson, and he took me immediately away from that hotel and hid me in the country and we make arrangement to prepare this hiding place. I will be kidnaped, he says, if these men discover the true state of things. These, he said, were the agents of the terrible man you call 'The Eel.'"

"He doubtless knew what he was talking about. Half a million. It would make a pretty ransom payment. And you couldn't even call in the Federals."

A muted telephone bell rang softly, a startling sound in this eerie place. Stephanie opened a cabinet, took the instrument. Her face relaxed when the caller spoke. She laughed oddly, amused.

"For you, Dex Ward."

"Who'd call me here?"

"Your so good friend and employer. Who else?"

Teverson was curt over the wire. Ward told him, "Certainly everything's all right. We had a little brush with some unexpected trouble on the way, but we cleared it up. Tell you later. What's on your mind?"

"I want you back here."

"More trouble?"

"Not immediately. I'm going out, but you be here, on hand, in case."

"I get it. Very well. I'll be along."

Ward was grinning a little as he turned away.

Stephanie said, "He is impatient, this Teverson?"

"Oh, quite!"

Their eyes met, and then hers slid away and she suppressed a giggle. She was suddenly twenty again, a little girl tickled and thrilled by the jealousy of men.

Ward looked at her, and as he looked the amusement

slowly died in him. The fun was hers, not his. If Teverson were jealous—doubtless it was his right. He became a little grim as he looked at her. Out of nowhere, for the first time, came a resentment, the smoldering willful rebellion of the male shut out. He did not like it.

As if aware, Stephanie patted the settee beside her. "Come and talk some more, Dex Ward. You have said nothing to me at all."

"That's just as well," he said shortly. "If you'll order out that boat, I'll be on my way. I've got orders."

She gauged his mood as stubborn, and came to him. Her lovely eyes were full of instant appeal. "Have you no hope for me, Dex Ward? I have laid before you all my plans. Can you say nothing?"

He slipped into his coat, pulled on gloves, deliberately. "I can say nothing now. I have a germ of an idea I'd be glad to offer. But not until I look into it. How may I get in touch with you in a hurry?"

She went to a desk and wrote the telephone number on a slip of paper. "If I am not here, you will leave a message. I will find you then."

"You'll hear from me."

"You really think there is something possible?"

"Can't say. I'll do my best."

"Oh, my poor people!" It was a prayer as she uttered it. She clutched gently at his coat lapels. "I shall be grateful. With all my life I shall be indebted to you."

HE STARED INTO her eyes. He stood very still, expressionless, and his own eyes were fluid with emotion. He took a deep breath and drew away.

"Call your minions, Madame Gorda, and speed the traveler. I've a raft of things to do in a hurry."

She laughed a short, rather shaky laugh, and went to the door, where she touched a bell button. "They are below. The boat will be ready to take you in two minutes."

During the ride back Ward figured out his immediate campaign. The cab that carried him across the bridge again into Manhattan finally deposited him at the door of the handsome and spacious Colonial Club on West Fifty-fifth Street. He looked at the board, grunted with satisfaction, and telephoned to the room of one Macdonald Sevier, who agreed to meet him at the bar in five minutes.

"Guns?" said Sevier, a stocky, executive type of man, a contemporary of Ward's. "Cannon? Rifles? Machine guns? What, and how many? And where?"

"Machine guns are the best bet. Light machine rifles chiefly. New or used, so long as they work when needed. Several hundred, I'd say. And export, of course."

"Export where?"

"Need I state? I'd as soon not."

Sevier pursed his lips. "No, I reckon you needn't. Anything can be arranged. Nobody looks closely at what's going out, so long as the money's coming in. You can even ship the stuff in some out of the way port in, say, Central America. Can be arranged, if absolutely necessary."

"I doubt it. Now how much per gun? And per ten thousand rounds of ammunition?"

Sevier frowned. "I'm in the steel business, Dex, and I can quote you anything from a second-hand battleship to a hairpin, but machine guns are something else. Let's sit down at a table and figure this out on paper."

In a little while, a memorandum in his pocket teeming with figures, Ward dashed in a taxicab to the Hotel Washburn across the town. A phone call had paved the way, and a tall, eccentric looking and lazily humorous young man awaited him in his room.

"A flying job?" he said. "Hell, I'll fly a washboard if you'll give me an engine! And I was raised in an amphibian."

"Hold on, Jerry. Fold up the humor tonight. I want facts and in a hurry. Can two or three amphibians be loaded in a ship's hold, and given calm weather, assembled on deck at sea, and put in the water to take off with a heavy load of freight?"

"Well… don't see why not. What kind of freight?"

"This is in strict confidence. Guns."

The pale eccentric eyes began to glow. "Guns?… Dex, you're talking business now. Let's have it."

THERE FOLLOWED MUCH technical talk, and considerable telephoning of a guarded nature, ascertaining that a total of four highly skilled and thoroughly reckless pilots were at liberty and open to a good proposition. It was very late when Ward finally headed homeward. He felt confident that his reception, if Teverson preceded him home, would be a bit frigid, but he was prepared.

Despite the lateness of the hour, several men lounged in the quiet Hotel Blassingame lobby. Ward darted for an elevator and rose rapidly to the tower. The elevator operator wore a peculiar look, but uttered no word. The cage stopped at his floor, and Ward stepped into the private foyer.

He was met by a sonorous volume of sound. Teverson was home—and playing the piano. He played the much abused *Prelude in C Sharp Minor* of Rachmaninoff, and he rendered it with a macabre suggestion of ferocity. With a peculiar sensation along his spine, Ward walked into the apartment.

He was struck motionless. The place was a shambles. Furniture was overturned, rugs were scattered, upholstery was ripped open. Desk and table drawers and their contents were strewn over the floor.

Across the great room Teverson sat behind the grand piano. He continued to play the thunderous chords. Ward strode over to him.

"What in hell's happened?"

Teverson spun about.

"Why weren't you here?"

"I was delayed. On business."

Teverson swore, with passion and rage. "Your business was here!"

Ward was silent an instant. Teverson had him—to a degree. "Nevertheless it was business. And no damned two-timing, I'll make a point of adding. I don't like the implications."

"Implications?" roared Teverson. He jumped up, grabbed Ward's arm. "Come here. Is that an implication?"

In the doorway leading to the serving pantry Ward stood frozenly staring. On the floor, in a welter of blood, lay the gaunt, grotesque body of Ali, his features fixed in final agony. From his body protruded the haft of a heavy knife.

"We had visitors while you were pursuing your blasted business!" snarled Teverson. "This is what I found, returning. I haven't checked up yet to see what they've discovered or made off with."

"Ali!" said Ward. "The poor devil!"

"And that's not all, sweetheart. Lay an eye to this."

Ward took the early edition of the morning newspaper Teverson handed him.

It was folded to display a large front page photograph— an odd thing indeed, the enormously enlarged reproduction of a fingerprint. Beneath it was the caption:

DO YOU KNOW THIS MAN?

This is the perfect fingerprint found by the police on a whisky glass in the fiat of Jessie Wilson, 17 Calvert Street, following the brutal murder of the girl three nights ago. This newspaper is broadcasting the print in the hope that the capture of the murderer may thus be expedited. *Who is this man?*

Ward said, "Well? Who is it?"

"I followed my hunch, sweetheart," Teverson said venomously, "and I dusted the glass in your bathroom with a little fingerprint powder of my own. I made expert comparison under magnification and I find—an exact duplicate of that photograph!"

"Duplicate?" Ward looked at his thumb instinctively.

"Since when have you taken to murdering your women?"

6

HIDE-AWAY

"HAVE YOU A set of fingerprints in any police file anywhere?" Horror crept coldly over Dex Ward. He tried to recall. "I tried driving a taxicab for a while. They took my prints when I applied for the hack license."

Teverson suddenly turned away and sat down. "Did you do it?"

"No!"

Teverson was silent. "Dex, I'm afraid. Jules Koerner has run us down. I can't imagine how, but he's done it at last. He knew I had a racket, and a rich one, but he could never figure it out. I think he's finally doing it. He's a man obsessed. Not only with breaking me, but rubbing me out. He's got men planted downstairs now, I know. They let me walk in. Leaving will be another matter. They're waiting. It's a corner."

Ward stared at him. "So what?"

"So far as I can see—the cops. They'll ruin me, they'll try to break you. But they're the only ones who can handle this. Better get headquarters on the phone."

"Why?"

"I tell you it's a corner!"

Dex Ward laughed. He went to a cabinet and got a decanter of whisky. He poured a stiff drink.

"Here, put this inside you. You need it. Hell, we're walking out of here right now, together."

Teverson looked at him opaquely.

Ward said, "Empty out the wall safe. They didn't crack that. Take your papers and money and a couple of guns and we'll get started."

"How? Through a coal chute?"

"Through the front lobby."

"Front lobby? They'll carry you out looking like something that went through a meat chopper."

"They will not! Those punks will be at every back door and coal chute in the hotel. We're taking the elevator to the mezzanine. From the mezzanine we're walking down to the lobby by way of the little stairs right by the front door. And out. It's a natural."

Teverson thought, sat erect, snapped a finger sharply. "Maybe you're right, maybe it can be done!" He paused, looked oddly, intently at Ward. "You'll do, fellow!" he added cryptically. "We'll try it."

They hurried. They stuffed pockets with papers and money and guns. A quantity of stuff discarded they piled in the fireplace and ignited. Then they walked out to the foyer and called the elevator. Dex Ward whistled as they waited.

The escape from the hotel was executed like a maneuver well rehearsed and unbeatable. The mezzanine, with its writing desks and lounges, was darkened and deserted. The inconspicuous stairs were partly concealed by a bank of potted palms. The door was but a few steps from the foot of the stairs. They walked calmly, quietly, down the stairs and out the door without attracting the attention of any of the grim watch whose eyes, over unread newspapers, were fixed on the elevators and the main stairs.

A night-owl taxicab line was parked at the door. No one was on watch at the door. They climbed into the head cab, ordered the driver to speed away, heading downtown. The cab moved, they were off.

They gazed back through the rear window.

A MAN AT the corner of the huge hotel building came running to the curb, to stare in uncertainty at the departing taxi. An instant, and he abruptly whistled shrilly. Other men came on the run. A cab was hailed, boarded, and set out at top speed.

"Turn east!" Ward commanded. "Come on—hell for breakfast through to Sixth Avenue!"

The driver, startled, obeyed. They sped through the side street.

"This corner to the right," said Ward. "That's it. Now fill in at the tail end of that cab line. Quick! And stand there."

Half a dozen taxis dozed at the curb, waiting patiently for the infrequent but highly profitable rides of early morning. Their taxi filled in behind the last cab. Ward slid from the seat, pulled Teverson to the floor, out of sight. The driver sat like a statue.

In a moment they heard a squealing of tires on a speeding turn. An engine roared, flew past, and was gone. Ward looked up and out. The pursuing taxicab was flying down Sixth Avenue in blind search.

"Step on it, driver!" snapped Ward. "Cut around and head uptown."

The man came to life. The cab backed, swung a half circle, and raced uptown. Ahead lay the deep green darkness of Central Park. They crossed Central Park South full speed and dived into the concealing shadows of the broad smooth drives. No pursuer followed.

Teverson sat back, lighted a cigarette. "Where did you get the shot in the arm?" he asked dryly.

"Maybe from Stephanie. I had a little practice at this earlier tonight."

"Tell me about it."

Ward related their experience with the big dark sedan downtown, the furious chase and almost miraculous escape.

"Hm," said Teverson. "That's certainly one way of promoting quick acquaintance."

Ward looked at him, shrugged. "Well, so what?"

"Nothing, nothing. Skip it. I dare say I've been collecting a few odd jitters myself tonight. Now tell me what kept you so long."

Ward debated how best to answer. He decided to lay his cards down and have it out on that basis. He told Teverson all he had learned from Stephanie, and all he had done in consequence."

"I don't know why you haven't thought of it, or what obstacles you have in mind that I'm not acquainted with, Tev. It occurred to me that mail is regularly delivered from ships a hundred miles at sea. Why not guns? The heavier load is no obstacle, in the right kind of plane. If the pilots pick out an unfrequented bit of coast to cross over, the authorities of the intervening nation needn't even be aware.

"The flights can be announced by short wave radio to those folks in the hills, and a landing place prepared. The ships can make as many air trips by night as necessary, climbing up into the substratosphere for greater secrecy. I can get the stuff, the planes, the pilots. Stephanie can arrange the cooperation at the other end. It's up to you. Can you provide the ship and a closemouthed crew?"

TEVERSON MULLED OVER the proposal. "How about costs?"

"All figured. A fair and honest price for the costs and risk involved should net you one hundred thousand clear."

"Me?"

"Certainly. I'm working for you."

"That's so," drawled Teverson. "I'd forgotten."

Ward paused. "You're feeling damned sarcastic tonight, aren't you?"

"I have a right to feel any way I want to tonight." Something bitter was lodged in the man's brain. "You know all my business now, so there's no need to keep it back. I had a shipment of rather priceless items from the estate of the late Duke of Magenta switched on me for a few packages of old iron. Two gold chalices, a reliquary, a crown and tiara—all loaded with jewels. The trustees of the Metropolitan would go crazy at sight of them, not to speak of the sheer intrinsic value. It was rather a blow."

"Who did it?"

"Our friend, Jules Koerner. The Eel, if you will. My man was knifed, carrying it ashore. The fellow with him escaped back to the ship; he told me the story tonight. He brought me the other packages. I don't know if they had more elaborate plans, or if it's merely The Eel's grotesque sense of humor, but the old iron, all carefully wrapped, was found with the body."

"Why do you have that stuff smuggled? It's in the art and antique classification surely. There's no bar to free entry."

"There'd be damned quick bar to free exit across the pond, I can tell you, if more was known of what I've done. I have agents in every foreign capital. Most of them I've never even seen, but I've got to protect them." Teverson raised his voice. "Driver, head for Harlem. Peter's Restaurant on 133rd."

They ordered ham and eggs, seated in a deep booth in a first rate restaurant in colored Harlem. It was the last place on earth to be observed by anyone they did not care to meet. They had dismissed the cab, cut loose from their last tie with the hotel. They ate hungrily, and talked. It was serious talk, for crisis was full upon them.

Ward said, "Why did you keep this racket of yours secret from me for so long, Tev?"

Tev snorted, "I'll tell you some time."

"Have it your way! And so what next? What's going to happen to it?"

"I've sent cables, cancelling all transactions for the present. Too dangerous. The Eel has found a good thing and he's not going to let it go."

"And what do you propose to do about that?"

Teverson chewed in silence a moment. "What would you suggest?"

"You've talked hard talk often enough. I should think you'd have a few ideas."

"Ideas? Plenty! But none of them is any good. I have no scruples and less squeamishness, but what are you going to do with a man who can't be found, is never seen, whose whereabouts and ways not even Walter Winchell can tell?

I never built up an organization of mugs and guerrillas because I've never needed them. I don't operate that way. My men are scattered on forty waterfronts. I've been facing The Eel alone, dodging him successfully for almost two years. It's like dodging a steam roller and finally getting one foot caught."

"I wish you'd told me sooner!" Ward said grimly. "I'd have picked up one of those mugs I met the other night and taken him along. I'd have asked him a few pertinent questions."

"Do you think he'd talk?"

"By the time I was through persuading him, he'd be so anxious to talk he'd take to reciting the multiplication tables backwards and forwards!"

TEVERSON LOOKED AT Ward, smiled sardonically, then wiped his mouth and threw down the napkin. "Come on, we'll get going."

"Where now?"

"You'll see."

On the way downtown in the cab, Ward leaned back and let his body relax. Teverson was silent. Suddenly Ward said, "How about the shipment of arms to Berengaria? Is it a go?"

"Well… I'll leave it to you. It's your job."

"The hell it is. I want a ship, and you're going to provide that."

"I'll find you the ship. You do the rest."

"Then it's a deal." Ward subsided, half dozing, his body rocking with the motion of the cab.

Nearing their destination, Ward was wide awake again. His curiosity was aroused, not to speak of a strong personal interest. They were again on the waterfront, this time on South Street along the East River, where the gleaming lights of the soaring bridges were like jeweled diadems set against the velvet darkness. The streets were deserted; the lamp posts, with their little orbits of empty illumination, stood isolated in the gloom. Here the damp air was heavy with the smell of tar and ancient timbers and the unforgettable, nostalgic smell of the harbor tides.

Teverson had the cab stop at a corner. The buildings facing the river wharfs were old stone and timber, or brick and timber, buildings dating before the Civil War. They were dingy, decayed, almost forgotten; they looked like a row of motionless ancient mariners dimly dreaming of the past.

Teverson waited till the cab had driven away, vanished. Then he led the way for two blocks. He paused before a three story stone house with a closed door, bleak grimy windows, and no sign of business of any kind. After a survey of the neighborhood, he quickly unlocked the door, and they entered. The air was dead, musty.

Teverson struck a match. By its light he found a flashlight that hung from a nail on the wall. They were in a hallway, unlittered and bare, but dusty. Teverson led the way upstairs. He opened a door, groped for a wall switch, and flooded the place with light.

"Well, I'll be damned!" said Ward.

"Fixing up that place for Stephanie gave me an idea to do the same for myself," said Teverson. "I'm glad I did."

It was a compact, but thoroughly comfortable apartment, fully furnished. Evidence of Teverson's tastes were everywhere. There was a baby grand piano, for one thing.

The prints on the walls were patently his choice, catholic and all embracing—an etching of Mont St. Michel hung across the room from an exquisite nude. The room was, for a building this size, truly enormous.

An upper floor had evidently been removed, and the ceiling rose to a high skylight, which eliminated the need of windows. A balcony and stairs gave access to upper rooms to the rear. A most practical impulse had inspired the place, but self-indulgence and self-satisfaction had entered largely in its preparation.

"I'LL COME TO the core of the matter at the outset," said Teverson. "Bear this in mind. There are three exits to this place. The front door will be used sparingly; it's better left closed. There's a rear door leading on a small fenced yard. The fence has a door in it, too. It leads directly through the adjoining yard to the rear of a tottering old tenement that opens on the street beyond. The tenement is condemned and vacated, but not locked. You will come and go that route principally. Now come and see the third exit."

Teverson walked through a compact kitchen in the rear. In a corner of the room an old closet projected. He opened the door and pointed downward. The closet had no floor, and Ward peered down where the flashlight beam penetrated the pit-like darkness. It went down a considerable distance, and the light glistened on a polished white-metal column like a stout pipe running through the center of the shaft from the top clear to the bottom. Ward guessed its use at once. It was like the brass poles in firehouses, used for instantaneous descent from upper floors.

"This is for emergency escape," Teverson explained. "You'll notice that this door and door frame are reinforced with steel. You'll notice further that the door cannot be opened unless you touch this spring when you turn the knob." He indicated an inconspicuous place in the closet wall close to the knob. "That's to hold up pursuit, if any. Since I was making preparations, I made them thorough. A slide down that chromium pole will drop you in a hole, alongside which runs an old brick line of sewer, abandoned years ago. I've explored it, so I know it's practical. That sewer leads to the river, running about one hundred yards and opening just above high water directly beneath an old ferry slip which is no longer in use. I picked this place carefully. We could almost resist a siege here to begin with, and if pressed, can make a quick, sure get-away. What do you think of it?"

"You must have had yourself rather a holiday fixing it all up!"

Teverson smiled. "Something like that." He added, "But it wasn't for a holiday I laid it out."

When they returned to the great room in the front, the skylight was a misty gray with the first light of dawn.

Ward, occupying a room off the upper balcony, was up and urgently awake after three hours' sleep, profound and dreamless. He looked in on Teverson, awakened him.

"Go ahead about your business," Teverson told him. "I'm sleeping it off. I've got to stay under cover anyway."

"What are you going to do about the killing in the apartment? Let it slide?"

"I'm going to stay under cover. Later I'll telephone Inspector Dineen and give him my side of the story in full, and he can do what he wants with it."

"They'll trace the call, Tev."

Teverson shook his head. "They cannot trace dial phone calls. Now you run along. Take note of the phone number. There are extra keys on a table out there, front and rear. Line up your proposition, and I'll supply the cash when it's ready."

"How about food?"

"Got enough canned stuff below to stock a grocery. Beat it and let a guy sleep!"

7

MILITARY PURCHASES

THE MORNING WAS a busy one—and not a little of a jittery one. The police had Ward's fingerprint tied up to one killing, and his description to another. He doubted that they had any line on his name or identity. The Colonial Club, the Hotel Washburn, and sundry offices he visited were not likely places to encounter trouble, but the sight of a strolling, watchful blue uniform on the street, or the accidental stare of a solid looking man in a crowded subway car, had the power to cause a little cringing dangerous fury to rouse inside him.

The business details were readily arranged when Ward talked in terms of ready cash. Five hundred guns of various types were available for almost immediate shipment. Three million rounds of ammunition lay waiting an order. Four Pelican amphibian planes, designed for staggering loads, could be delivered that very day if required. Ward assembled his flying acquaintance, Jerry, and the three other volunteers, and held a conference which satisfied everybody.

It was noon when he telephoned Stephanie. He spoke guardedly, but emphatically. She understood, and was ecstatic, half squealing her joy, half weeping her intense relief.

"Oh, that is wonderful, Dex Ward! It is the deliverance of my country. It is the saving of my father's life. You must tell me more. I must hear all about it. There is much I must do."

"I'll call you later. I'd better warn you. This will kill that half million!"

"It is well killed. It is—what you call?—a one shot. A grand magnificent one shot worth too many millions to count."

"We'll talk it over," Ward promised.

When he returned to the hide-out, Ward found Teverson in a mood. He was at the piano, playing softly; playing, Ward felt, almost morbidly. Ward would have felt better if he heard again the crashing chords of anger, fury.

Teverson listened to Ward's account of the morning's accomplishments. Without a word then he got up, disappeared in his room, and returned with a sheaf of crisp treasury notes. He handed them to Ward, who counted them. There were fifty one-thousand-dollar bills.

"That will start you," Teverson said. "Stephanie will have to lay it on the line now. And you'll have to risk going over to Duff Garry's this afternoon. I can't locate Captain Carnigan. He's the man I want if possible; he owns his own ship, and his crew is acid-tested. Tell Garry to keep an eye open for him, and to pass the word quietly in the proper places. If Carnigan's got a cargo and has cleared, Garry will know."

"Do you want me to give him the phone number for Carnigan?"

"Absolutely not. Arrange a meeting. Tonight at eleven, or tomorrow night. Anywhere you choose. You make the contact first, phone me, and I'll come and complete the deal with Carnigan."

Ward went out. He was uneasy. Something was wrong, and he could not put his finger on it. It was not trouble, which was definite, measurable, something to cope with. It was more insidious.

HE RODE IN a cab up the Bowery, proceeding slowly, watching out the window. Finally he ordered the cab to halt. He got out, entered a restaurant and bar, and ordered a drink. The window bore the fantastic name of "Ritz-Waldorf Bar & Grill." It was a capacious, deep place, with tables and large booths. A raffish, bleary crowd patronized the bar. He finished the drink and went out and proceeded onward in the cab. He rode to West Street, got out, walked three blocks, and with his vigilance on edge strolled into Duff Garry's place on Calvert Street.

Garry chuckled deep in his barrel body as he shook hands.

Ward said, "Coast clear? Anybody here?"

"Nobody now, son. You scared them all away! How's Tev?"

Ward delivered his message, and Garry listened attentively, nodding full comprehension.

"Tev is laying low, Garry. You'll know why. I'll leave it to you to get word to Captain Carnigan. At eleven tonight I'll be in the Ritz-Waldorf bar on the Bowery. I'll wait an hour. If nobody shows up, I'll do the same tomorrow."

"Right! I'll take care of it. Carnigan's visiting relatives in the country or something. He's due around."

Ward got out of the neighborhood fast as possible, and without any untoward encounter. He returned to the hideout. For the moment, there was no more to do but wait.

Something like a wire suddenly tensing drew taut in Ward as he entered the old house. He listened. Tev was talking. He was talking to Stephanie, and she was laughing, talking, sighing in happiness. In the small kitchen Ward stood still for a time. He could not hear them distinctly, except for an occasional word.

Ward could not understand the feeling which held him now as in the grip of a vise. He did not want it, loathed it, would flee from it if he could, but he could not. It had him. It was irrational, akin to hatred, to some form of insanity. It took a reasonable, wholly occupied and balanced human being, and in an instant tripped his senses and confounded his faculties and made a complete fool of him. And knowing it, he could do nothing about it.

He was jealous! Passionately, madly jealous.

He strode into the front room. Stephanie was seated deep in a huge red leather upholstered chair, Teverson was striding up and down the room. Teverson was afire, it shone in his eyes, and his earlier mood was gone. They greeted Ward enthusiastically—and yet his entry dissipated something that had been there before he strode in. Stephanie gazed at him, gazing as if her eyes would say more than her tongue said. Teverson cooled a little, and shot questions at Ward about Garry, about Carnigan.

I'll take care of it," Ward told him. "We get together tonight, or perhaps tomorrow night if there's delay."

Stephanie said, "There will be no delay in the shipment? That will go soon, Dex?"

"Soon as we get the ship and load it. I'm holding back definite orders only until the ship is settled. We can see her clearing out to sea inside a week, with luck."

"Mr. Teverson has been telling me all the details. I shall arrange a message to go through in code to my father with this good news. How long do you think this ship will take to arrive in position to send off the planes?"

WARD GLANCED AT Teverson, and he said, "Carnigan's old tub will take at least two weeks to get within striking distance. There will be other factors. If there are any warships in the vicinity, Carnigan will be forced to continue on and return later. I'd tell your father, Stephanie, not to look for anything before three weeks—but to count on it with fair certainty within six."

She sat back and dreamed of triumphs to come.

Teverson asked Ward, "Did you bring any papers?"

Ward swore at himself. "I never even gave them a thought!"

"Hm! Hadn't you better go get them?"

Ward grabbed his hat and hurried out the rear way. He bought three newspapers at a local stand. He glanced through them, returning. He found the story on page three. There was a note of bewilderment in the account of the murder in the Hotel Blassingame. Burglary was evident. The Arab servant victim, on testimony of hotel employees, had returned to the hotel at a time when both other occupants of the suite were out. He was presumed to have surprised the burglars, and been slaughtered in consequence. So much seemed clear. The mystery lay in the disappearance of the two masters of the apartment. They had come in separately, they must have discovered the slain man—and they had thereafter vanished without even reporting the crime. The police sought them for questioning.

Teverson said, reading the stories, "I wonder just how much the police know about this. They haven't told the reporters everything they found. They have used the phony names without question."

"What was there to find of importance?" Ward asked.

Teverson grinned, baring his teeth slightly. "They could find what I found. If it occurs to them to compare fingerprints!"

Ward made a face, wryly. "That's so!" He pondered. "Look here. Where could I lay hands on some old clothes? Very old, shabby, ragged."

"There's a pile of junk in the cellar left from the time this place was cleaned up."

Stephanie, frowning, said, "What for do you want old clothes?"

Teverson said dryly, "They want him for murder. They found a little street-walker dead after Dex paid her a visit."

Stephanie reddened a little and said seriously, "You wish to tell me about this, Dex?"

"Certainly!" snorted Ward, with an angry glance at Teverson. He curtly related his adventure—and misadventure—on Calvert Street, and told what came of it. "I doubt if there's a conviction in the evidence, but there'd be an unholy time with the police regardless. If I'm going to he running around this part of New York, I've got to take on a bit of protective coloration. The old clothes will help."

Stephanie was thoughtful. She looked like a woman who

was aware by intuition of something important, something she knew was there yet which eluded her.

Teverson, looking somewhat thoughtful himself, sat down at a desk and scrawled a note which he inserted in an envelope and addressed.

"You won't need any old clothes for this, Dex. Deliver that for me. Right away."

Ward looked at him opaquely, looked at the envelope. "Very well. Business?"

"Important business!"

Ward took Stephanie's hand briefly in leaving. He did not know if it were actuality, or merely his blind instinctive desire, but he thought he detected a pressure against his hand, an anxious secret flash of wordless communication in the brilliance of her eyes. Worse, he did not know if this were wantonness, duplicity, or necessary diplomatic expedient. He felt sullen anger.

8

ON THE BOWERY

THE ERRAND TOOK Ward to the upper East Side, to that quiet, austere neighborhood of aristocratic residence just off Fifth Avenue. The street number was that of a huge and grotesque pile of granite and bronze and copper which had been, a generation before, the palatial residence of a newly, crazily rich man who had come out of the West to lay siege to New York society—and who had thrown up his dreams for the love of the wife of a business rival, with whom he had run off to Europe.

The house was empty and closed for years, until an equally powerful millionaire bought it to shelter his fabulous private collection of jewels, art treasures, and incunabula. The man whose name Teverson had written on the envelope was the much envied curator of this private museum, Dr. Beecher.

Ward was forced to explain his wishes to a plainclothes agency detective outside the bronze gates, to a uniformed doorman, and finally to a severe, businesslike young woman at a desk inside. He refused to surrender the envelope to anyone but the person to whom it was addressed. He was admitted to a small office of paneled oak and Georgian English furnishings, where a quizzical, bespectacled small man with bushy gray hair and a scholarly air of erudition smiled a welcome from behind his desk.

"Sorry it was necessary to disturb you, sir," said Ward, warming to the smile. "I gather the matter is important enough to be stubborn about it."

Dr. Beecher opened and read the letter in silence. He rubbed his jaw and read it again. "Hm! And why is it so important?"

"I don't know. I haven't read it."

"He merely notifies me that he will have nothing of interest to show me for an indefinite period, and that I will do nothing to try to get in touch with him until I hear from him. That's rather unnecessary. I've been hoping to hear from him with news of something new and extraordinary, and thought this might be it."

"We're shut down for a while, Doctor. Force of circumstances. He probably sent that message in order to give me something to do."

The curator stared at him. "I've never seen you before. You're in his confidence, of course?"

"Naturally."

"Tell me something about yourself, won't you? Teverson is such an extraordinary man! Half scholar, wholly adventurer. He is an historical piece himself. I've wondered about his associates. You don't mind my interest, do you?"

Ward laughed. Here was a man, secure as Gibraltar in life, who doubtless read detective stories every night in bed, who thrilled vicariously to the melodrama he imagined in the life of a man like Teverson. His curiosity was artless, and Ward obliged, regaling him with a lurid account of himself. He drew broadly on his imagination with easy conscience, wondering what would be the man's reaction to the gruesome truth.

They visited for almost an hour. To Ward's amusement and delight, tea was served—tea and scones and marmalade and strawberry preserve. It made little sense, this cloistered ceremony, in the midst of Ward's violent existence, but it was a valued and most amiable interlude.

"I appreciate this very much, my boy," Beecher said as Ward took his leave. "I hope you'll drop in again for a chat. I might even say…" He hesitated, smiled, reddening a little, boyishly. "I might go so far as to say that I'd appreciate it even more if you were to conduct me on a little tour some evening when you're not engaged."

"Where?"

"WHY, I'VE ALWAYS been curious about the Bowery, now. Who hasn't? I've merely seen it from an automobile window speeding through to the Bridge. I've never had the temerity to investigate it at first hand. Tell me—is it really as tame today as it is reported to be?"

"I'm afraid so, Doctor." Ward smiled. But thought flashed quickly in his mind. This old boy might be very useful. The rendezvous at the Ritz-Waldorf was an uneventful business engagement. There'd be no harm. He said suddenly, "Are you busy this evening, Doctor?"

"No."

"Would you care to help me keep an engagement on the Bowery? With one of Teverson's sea captains? It should afford good opportunity to see it from the inside."

The good doctor stared, then his eyes glowed. "Why, delighted! No end delighted, my boy. Will you have dinner with me?"

"I'm afraid not. But you do this. Be at the Brevoort at ten. I'll pick you up. We'll walk to the Bowery and see the sights. If I meet my man, it may be necessary for me to ask you to call it an evening and leave. You won't mind?"

"Not a bit. I'll be there at ten." Ward half regretted the impulse as he returned downtown. He took the subway; there was a long wait, and the train, when it came, was crowded. He swayed, hanging on a strap, and mulling over many problems.

Risky or not, this Dr. Beecher was a contact he wanted cultivated, and quickly. Since he was irretrievably in this racket, he wanted to know the ropes. He felt uneasy about Teverson. Teverson seemingly begrudged information, yet expected much of his bodyguard. The man was unfathomable. And his present moodiness was truly disturbing. Ward wondered, could the man be losing his nerve, his grip?

The message to Dr. Beecher was plainly a stratagem, conceived on the instant for a purpose. The purpose was to get Ward out of the way while Stephanie was there. It was not like Teverson. Ward could understand the motive, but not the act. He could appreciate the cold threat of a bullet, but not petty, transparent wiles.

The heavy man hanging on the strap adjoining Ward's lost balance, lurched, and his weight pressed heavily against Ward. Ward stiffened, irritated at the awkwardness, but saying nothing. The man recovered balance without apology, and stared stonily at the car advertisements overhead. The train slowed to pull into a station.

Then the heavy man rasped from the side of his mouth, very quietly, "Listen, you! You're getting off at this station.

I'm going with you. I don't want any trouble in this car. Start any, and I'll finish it. If you're wise you'll go quietly."

Ward stared. "What in hell's burning you up?"

"That gun under your arm, brother. I want to have a talk with you about it. My police shield's in my pocket, and I'll show it to you outside—if you insist."

The man gazed directly, icily, into Ward's hot stare. And Ward felt against his body the hard metallic pressure of a revolver held in the big man's pocket.

WARD MOVED WHEN the doors opened. Hot fury was like scalding waves sweeping over him. The big man was close on his heels. They pushed through the press of passengers to the platform. Ward walked slowly, the man a little to his rear. The train doors closed, it glided off, rumbling, and was gone with diminishing roar.

"Stop right here," the heavy man commanded.

Ward faced him. "Don't touch me. Show me the shield."

A sneering smile touched the mouth of the man. His right hand was buried in his coat pocket. He reached with his other hand into an inside pocket.

Quicker than vision, Ward slapped hard at the pocketed gun, shoved, jamming the hand there; immediately grabbed the man's right elbow, jerked on it powerfully. There was an explosion; the bullet struck the cement floor. The man, with a sharp cough of astonishment and pain, was spun completely about on his heels by that agonizing wrench. He tried to pull the gun out, but his shoulder was momentarily paralyzed.

Ward sprinted for the far end of the station platform.

The man raised instant hue and cry. People on the platform stood wide-eyed, fixed in attitudes of impartial amazement. No one interfered with Ward. He dropped grimly from the platform to the tracks and raced head-long down the cavernous tunnel. Before him the red light of the departed train winked smaller and smaller. On the other track an uptown train was approaching. He glanced hastily over his shoulder; already another downtown train, close on the heels of the first because of some unscheduled delay of the latter, was coasting as it neared the station. It was a snarl of trains.

Ward swore with vehement satisfaction. The heavy man back on the platform stood waving his revolver in his left hand, yelling down the tunnel at his escaped prisoner. But he dared not set in pursuit, with the tracks crowded with trains. Ward stepped between the two lines of tracks, where the line of iron-girder uprights buttressed the tunnel, and he waited.

The uptown train passed with a blast of wind just as the downtown was pulling into the station. Ward stepped into the uptown tracks. He was concealed from view of the heavy man by the trains. He gauged his chances, and sprinted again, all speed, back toward the station on the uptown side, parallel to his first course.

The heavy man evidently made appeal to the motorman of the train at his platform; the tunnel suddenly quivered with ear-shattering sound of the train whistle blowing for help. It was a sound audible even up on the street, one that brought every policeman within hearing on the run.

Ward gained the end of the uptown platform, mounted the narrow ladder. He walked, fast but with deliberation, toward the exits half way up the platform. Passengers just discharged from the train stood stock still, looking at one another in fright. A number looked at Ward, but no one did anything. He was smiling slightly, a hard crooked smile, He strode through the turnstile and up the stairs.

On the avenue a street car was just getting under way. Ward ran, caught on, and boarded the car. He paid the fare, walked through to the front platform. He rode two blocks, and dropped off alongside a taxicab. He got into the cab and snapped, "Broadway! In a hurry."

The cab was off like a bolt, streaking crosstown to make the green lights that shone before them.

Ward took out a handkerchief, removed his hat, and wiped his forehead. Then he laughed.

TEVERSON AND STEPHANIE were both gone when Ward returned to the hide-out. He threw together a bit of lunch, read the newspapers, and was rummaging in the cellar, with a complete outfit of long discarded men's clothing assembled from the rubbish there, when Teverson came in. Ward laid the clothes aside and went upstairs.

"See Beecher?" Teverson asked.

"I did," tersely.

"Say anything?"

"Thanks and regards, that's all."

Teverson grunted. He sat down and opened a newspaper.

Ward said, "Did you take Stephanie home?"

"Went to the bank with her to transfer funds. Then I dropped her off at Regatta House uptown."

"What's there?"

"They have a yacht landing on the East River. For tenants in the house, and a few favored outsiders. She's one. She ties up that runabout there occasionally. Risky, but saves time."

Ward grunted. Conversation was scarce today. Getting on each other's nerves. Something. He looked into a mirror, feeling a day's growth of beard. He'd leave it there. It would go well in a day or two with the rags he had already in the cellar.

Rags! He frowned, wondering. Where was all this leading? Why was he involved in this fantastic career? He stood still, thinking. But all he could think of, numbly, was a pair of dark and brilliant eyes. He yawned suddenly, went in and stretched out on a couch, and was instantly asleep.

At ten that evening Ward got out of a taxicab at the Hotel Brevoort. He found Dr. Beecher waiting in the lobby, eyes twinkling and eager. They stopped off in the grill for a drink, and then set out walking. The upper end of the Bowery was only a few blocks east.

Ward watched the good doctor for signs of shock and repugnance as they strolled down the great wide Bowery, so soiled and disheveled, pathetic and sinister. The dingy shops, the verminous cheap eating places, the fetid old saloon, the stark, prison-like flophouses—these assuredly were as foreign as Mars to the gentle, cloistered Dr. Beecher.

Likewise the motley stream of humanity along the sidewalks—the reeling, mumbling drunks, the starved, half stupefied derelicts, the hunch-shouldered, desperate-eyed youngsters in from the roads and jungles of the nation. Ward watched for signs, and saw only a quiet intensity of gratification. It was not gloating, nor was it condescension or morbid curiosity. It was unconscious, unaffected: the man was honestly thrilled.

Ward knew that the doctor saw in this grim dumb-show of discouragement and defeat all that he conceived the Bowery to be, knew that his eye unwittingly passed over the small dapper knots of hard-faced loungers on the street corners, the occasional ferret-eyed and well-clothed passer-by whose furtive manner made so questionable his status here. There was much the good doctor did not see. Which was just as well.

It was going on eleven when they walked into the Ritz-Waldorf. Instantly Ward felt definite misgivings. Something was wrong, although he could not place it. The great bar-room was crowded, smoke-filled, acrid with stale beer and unwashed humanity. The crowd was a mixed and peculiar medley of types, stiffs and boes and local gamblers and types unrecognizable. Ward and the doctor walked through and stepped to the bar and ordered drinks. Ward, frowning slightly, studied the noisy, argumentative crowd in the bar mirrors.

THE DOCTOR WAS covertly inspecting the man alongside him at the bar. The fellow was about thirty, swarthy and black haired, sullen looking, husky and muscular. His thick eyebrows were a single line; his chin was sharply, oddly cleft. He was alone, and by his adequately sleek appearance, no Bowery drifter. He stared into his beer. Ward gave him a glance and looked further, making certain that no one likely to be Captain Carnigan waited anywhere alone.

Presently the doctor turned back to Ward, and in a low, confidential tone said, "This is most interesting. I could spend a week right here, studying these types. This fellow

"Don't stir a hand!"
Ward ordered

beside me—don't look now—take him, for instance. I have no idea why he's here, but there must be some extraordinary reason. He's a stonecutter. He plays the violin rather well, even though he's untutored. He was born in either Corsica or Sardinia, and was brought here at a very early age.

"He lives somewhere on the outskirts of the city on a bit of land where they keep goats and probably dig a small truck garden. He isn't married, and no doubt makes his home with some of his family, very likely his father, who runs the stone yard."

Ward stared at the doctor, stole a glance at the fellow next him, stared again. "What are you talking about?"

"I'm merely telling you about him. I can't find out any more."

"Where did you get all this information?"

"Why, my dear boy, it's written all over him. His hands. His clothes. Deduction, you know. Observation." Then he smiled disarmingly. "But perhaps my training of years as curator, establishing or rejecting the authenticity of objects of art by means of infinitely small observations gives me the advantage of you. I've always fancied myself as a detective of sorts, although I've never had opportunity to test my abilities in action. This man's hands, for instance—"

"Never mind. What did you say about extraordinary reasons for being here?"

The doctor shrugged. "It seems obvious. Such people are very clannish. They do not come to places like this without good reason. He is possibly waiting for someone."

WARD TOOK A deep breath and stared with a hard and calculating eye at the man along the bar. He let his gaze rove around the room. Clannish, eh? Why then didn't the fellow gang with the three seated at a table immediately adjoining the door? They were all of a type. Scattered around the big room there were others. They were more than all of a type—they were all similarly engaged. They were industriously doing nothing. They were waiting... waiting.

Ward turned all this over and over in his mind, coldly, very practically. He had no solid assurance of anything. He must proceed by sheer hunch—and proceed correctly. In the game Ward played these days there were no mistakes. A single mistake was one beyond the limit.

Ward sipped his drink, said, "Doc, wait here for me a minute."

He strolled away, walking to the back of the deep room where the washrooms were. He took note of the lights, high brilliant one-hundred-watt bulbs, glaring and undisguised. He observed the high windows in the rear, strongly barred with strips of steel. The booths in the rear were almost all occupied. He entered the washroom and was alone.

There was a single window here, also strongly barred. It would require tools and time to get through it. He stood motionless, thinking. The night was chill, and he swore softly, harshly, bitterly.

The three at the door. If they meant business, there was no getting by them. The remainder, scattered around, covered every quarter of the room. A corner!

Ward went outside and strolled slowly back to the bar, where the doctor was engrossed in conversation with a bleary individual who hoarsely averred his intention of remembering the doctor in his prayers for buying a poor thirsty man a drink. Ward leaned on the bar, called the bartender and ordered a round set up.

The bartender, inquiring the brand of Scotch preferred, side-stepped in response to a thumping in the floor underfoot. It was another bartender returning from tapping a fresh keg in the cellar; he raised up a trapdoor and climbed up out of it, dropping it in place.

Ward said, "Doc, let's sit down."

"Do you wish to? Very well."

Ward led the way. They carried the drinks. They found an empty table farther back, close by the open end of the bar. It was not very pleasant. One reeling reveler sprawled bodily into the doctor's lap, to his consternation and amusement. Ward shook his head. It was impossible either to shock or anger the doctor tonight. He was entirely too pleased with himself, his adventure. Ward felt a little ill at the responsibility on his own shoulders.

He watched, but still Captain Carnigan did not come.

No one came, that is, who could possibly match the description Ward had of the sailor.

"Doc," Ward said curtly, "I have some bad news for you. I want you to do exactly as I say, without question. We're in trouble, we're in a corner, and we're going to face a time getting out of it."

Beecher looked at him as if making certain it was no jest, then he smiled and said, "Yes? Go on." He smiled, but his gray eyes were flinty and undaunted.

"I'm going to get up and walk in the direction of the front door," said Ward. "You stay here. Don't watch me as I go. But get ready. If anything starts—a yell or a gunshot—dive behind that bar and open the trapdoor in the floor. Hold it open; the lights may go out. I'll come sailing straight for it. We'll both go down—you first, without delay. After that… we'll see. Got it straight?"

The doctor glanced from the corner of his eye at the floor in back of the bar, sized up the trapdoor, and nodded coolly. "I've got it, boy."

"I may be wrong." Ward got to his feet, expressionless. "We'll go see."

He strolled through the crowd and headed for the front door, whistling, absently adjusting the knot in his necktie. His right hand was close to his coat lapel. He looked directly at no one. There was a cold feeling in the pit of his stomach.

The three at the table beside the door slowly shoved back their chairs. The fellow at the bar casually turned about and leaned against it, elbows resting on the bar edge. No one looked at anyone else.

Next, one of those at the table got up. Another unfolded

a newspaper, placed it carefully on the table. His right hand was concealed under the paper.

Ward pulled out a cigarette, felt for a match. He glanced around, eyed the fellow standing back of the bar, requested the favor of a light. The man looked at him with jet opaque eyes, expressionless face. Slowly he took a book of matches from his pocket and extended them.

Ward reached for the matches—and gripped the wrist instead. He snapped hard, with all his weight behind the pull, jerked the fellow off his feet and swung him around in front, facing the door, holding him in a grip of paralyzing torture.

At the table, the newspaper was jerked away, and the man behind it raised an automatic, half squeezed, hesitated—was lost. Ward shot him between the eyes.

Ward backed to the bar. A fury raged in him. He ignored the mad panic that broke like thunder in the place. All too well that crowd knew the sound of guns, the smell of death. The stampede ruined the plans of the gang—that, and the human shield Ward held relentlessly before him.

Ward lined the automatic on the lights overhead. The shots were like a machine gun at a trifle slower tempo. The electric bulbs simply vanished, all in a row. The place was in pitch darkness, a mad, milling frenzy of terrified men and cursing, yelling gunmen.

Ward raised a knee and violently projected his prisoner from him. He vaulted over the bar, landing on a prostrate, trembling bartender. He felt for Dr, Beecher. The doctor was at his post, the trapdoor was raised.

"Down with you!" Ward ordered.

9

MASQUERADE

THEY SCURRIED BELOW, dropping the trapdoor. It shut them off from the riot, but the din of it was a minor thunder in the wooden ceiling over their heads.

Ward struck a match. He glanced sharply at Beecher. The man was positively glowing with excitement. There were no second thoughts in him, no weighing of consequences. Ward wondered if the man realized what was actually happening to him.

The cellar was a narrow, dank place, with racks of beer kegs and stout padlocked cabinets evidently used for storing bottled liquor. In the front, stone steps led up to flat iron doors level with the sidewalk. To the rear was darkness. Ward struck another match and walked back.

He found a stone wall, a door, and beyond, a furnace and coal bin. Still another door, made of steel and heavily barred and locked, but readily opened from within, gave on another steps and the rear yard. Quenching the match, Ward emerged silently into the yard.

Within the saloon, on the other side of the barred windows, a feeble glow of light shone; and the panic was subsiding. The rear yard was dark, quiet; there was no sign of life other than a few curious heads peering from nearby tenement windows, roused by the shouting and the stampede. Ward walked to the end of the yard, examined the fence there.

"I'll give you a boost, Doc. We'll have to scale it."

He helped the doctor up and over, then sprang up, caught the fence top and swung himself into the adjoining yard. The way was clear before them; the light of an open tenement hallway beckoned, and the street beyond.

Ten minutes later Ward and Dr. Beecher got out of a cab at the Brevoort and entered the grill. Ward immediately went to a telephone and called Teverson. There was no answer.

"My heavens," said the doctor when he returned, "I don't ordinarily take more than a drink or two at most of an evening, Ward, but I do badly need another now!"

Ward smiled a little, dryly, still tense himself. "You certainly saw life in the raw, Doc. More than I ever bargained to show you."

"But what was it all about? I saw you draw your pistol. Did you hit someone?"

"I did."

"Did you—?"

"Yes, I did. I got him before he got me. There was a whole gang planted there. The lad I shot was the trigger man; the others were in reserve. They wanted to get me near the door, so as to have the way clear for a quick getaway."

"But why is this?"

Ward shrugged. "Secrets of the trade, Doc. I suppose you've often bought things from Teverson, and paid well for them. Sometimes those things have cost more than money. They've cost human lives. The less said the better. You saw more tonight than I'd willingly have shown you."

The doctor was thoughtful. "I understand your reticence. I've often wondered. In fact, I've faced the necessity of rationalizing my own participation in dealings undeniably sub rosa, and believe I have done so. Human life seems to be one of the inescapable costs of all living, law-abiding, or otherwise."

"Hm! Pretty hardboiled, Doc, aren't you?"

Beecher shrugged. "My personal philosophy allows no fear of death. It is a phenomenon of life, and fear is super-stition. I had simply much rather you survived than the fellow whose life you so expertly ended."

Ward remembered something. "Tell me, Doc, how did you pick up all that information about the fellow standing next you at the bar?"

"Why, I took one detail and another and added them all up. There were visible traces of powdered stone in his fingernails, first of all, and in his thick eyebrows as well. Powdered stone has a definite consistency and color, differ-ent from talc or cement. The tips of the fingers of his left hand were calloused from the strings of a violin. On the back of his right hand he bore a tattooed symbol of the cross and stiletto, a superstitious practice among the more lawless hill folk of both Corsica and Sardinia."

"What makes you think he came here at an early age?"

"I JUDGED THAT he was brought here early in infancy because his ears were not pierced for earrings, as would certainly be the case if he had been brought up there as a child. The tattoo marking he would have had done of his own initiative as a youth in this country. I'm certain he lives on the city's outskirts. He had a number of the tiny thorns of the burdock clinging to his trouser legs, although he had neither mud nor yellow country dust on his shoes. He most likely uses well trodden short-cuts over weed-grown city lots.

"I noticed also that his shirt had once been torn and repaired at the collar, and the workmanship was typically that of a professional laundry seamstress, eliminating a thrifty wife and designating him as single."

"But what was an industrious fellow like that doing with a gun mob?"

"I've heard," Beecher suggested, "that gunmen often practice some honest trade intermittently for the sake of the alibi it affords. Stone cutting is no casual employment, but a highly skilled craft. It's likely that he was brought up in the trade, and quite possible that his family owns such a business. I'd look for him, if you're interested, in the neighborhood of such cemeteries as are patronized by his own kind."

Ward reflected, nodded. "The idea's worth trying. I know just the man for the job. I once worked for him. His name is Hymie Holtz, and he's one of the best private detectives in the business. I'll have to get you two together sometime."

Ward snorted and shook his head when he finally saw Dr. Beecher off in a taxi. The good doctor was beyond belief or comprehension! Ward went to the telephone and called Teverson again—with no better result. It was mystifying.

Ward got into another cab and rode East to Second Avenue, getting out at a large modern apartment house. There was a brisk exchange at the telephone switchboard inside, and then Ward rose in the elevator to a penthouse fourteen floors above the street. A stout stocky man in shirt sleeves, bald of head and blandly round of face, was waiting for him.

"Long time since I saw you, Ward. I've been looking for you at the office."

"I've been busy, Hymie. I've got business tonight that can't wait till tomorrow."

"Job?"

"Got one. I chucked the burlesque job for a rise in life."

"So they complained to me. You were a damned fool. You could have come back with me if you didn't like it. Hymie Holtz, Inc., will always talk job. I ain't so sure yet that you were made for the private detective agency business, but any guy that can combine the best features of a Park Avenue politician and a Tenth Avenue yegg is a handy guy to have around the place."

Ward grinned, dryly. "You're probably right about the detective angle, Hymie. I'm just a sucker for people. They ride all over me. I couldn't hurt a fly, and I didn't like the work. But I liked the burlesque job still less."

"And what you're doing now, selling bonds in Wall Street?"

"The nail right on the head, Hymie. Bonds."

"Well… I was a dope to listen to Morris Weiss when he begged me to let you go to work for his burlesque. I could use you. If you want a job you let me know."

"I will. In the meantime—I've got an assignment for the agency to handle in a hurry."

WARD TOLD HIM what he desired. To locate an unmarried, violin playing stone cutter, born in Corsica or Sardinia about twenty-five years ago. He gave a professional description of the subject and detailed everything else he could think of relating to him. Hymie imperturbably jotted down memoranda on a pad. For all his plaintive mildness, the man was uncanny in his results with the most difficult cases.

"This ain't so tough!" he remarked. "I got three men idle—I'll put them all on this tomorrow morning. With this information I could almost tell you his telephone number."

"I want that, and a few more details—soon as it can be done."

"I bet you I have it this time tomorrow night. What's your telephone number, so I can call you?"

"I'll call you."

The fat man looked at him. "So? No telephone? You ain't that broke, I can tell by looking. What is it?"

"I'm living with a friend, Hymie. This is personal business."

Hymie looked suspicious, then shrugged. "Okay—you call me tomorrow afternoon, and I'll tell you even what size collar this fellow wears."

Down on Second Avenue, Ward entered a drug store and tried a third time to get Teverson on the telephone. He waited while the receiver buzzed the call for four long minutes in vain. He came away frowning. What was wrong? Teverson had instructed him to call.

He debated speeding to the hide-out. But if Teverson weren't there, then the man wasn't there! Ward took another cab, riding uptown to Times Square, where he stopped at the cosmetic counter of a large drug store, carefully selecting a varied supply of theatrical make-up. He then ordered the driver to hasten downtown.

The place was in darkness when Ward let himself into the secret apartment. He looked around, but there was no sign of Teverson. He thought it over a moment, and then picked up the telephone and called Stephanie. A gruff male voice answered, to tell him that Madame Gorda was not at home.

Ward swore luridly.

Then he saw the note. It lay fiat on a small table.

Dex:—I'm going nuts, hanging around here! Must find out a few things. I've phoned Duff Garry to let me in the back way; must see him. Talked to Inspector Dineen—he offers immunity if I'll call at his home and give the lowdown. I dunno. If I'm not in, you'll hear from me. We can close the deal with Carnigan tomorrow.

Tev.

A cold, cold feeling stole over Dex Ward. Teverson should never have shown himself anywhere in town tonight. There was treachery abroad, and no way of knowing where it lay. Tonight he himself had been betrayed into the hands of the henchmen of The Eel, and Teverson was venturing into more than he could possibly conceive. And Stephanie....

WARD PUT THROUGH a call again to Brooklyn. He got the same gruff male voice, and demanded to know where Madame Gorda had gone.

"Is strict orders," said the man. "No can tell anybody. Is very sorry. Strict orders."

Ward told him to have her call if she returned within the half hour, and hung up. He paced up and down the room, intense of thought, groping for inspiration.

He made up his mind, and went down to the cellar and brought up the heap of shabby clothing. The fifty thousand dollars Teverson had entrusted to him, he hid behind a picture in his room. He spent all of half an hour in the bathroom under a strong light before the mirror, delicately plying scissors and razor and tweezers, and applying minute quantities of make-up. He worked inside his mouth, affixing wads of cotton in his cheeks where they would do the most good. He studied the effect, and worked some more, and studied it critically again, and finally was done. He slipped off his clothes and donned the raffish castoff costume. He took a look at himself in a full length mirror.

The total effect was eerie. To begin with, the shapeless clothes completely altered the lines of his muscular body. The grime and unbalanced coloration of his face, the darkened, altered eyebrows, the hollow cheeks and heavy-boned jaws, threw his features entirely out of focus. The growth of beard, a blackened stubble, helped considerably. And the final touch was the prominent eye-tooth now capped with gold, a glittering and most convincing counterfeit.

The transformation might not deceive so sharp an eye as that of Hymie Holtz. Nor of Teverson, or Stephanie. But a sharp eye would be truly needed to penetrate it at a glance. It would have to serve, however risky.

Ward strapped on his shoulder holster, slipped the .45 in a hip pocket, made a final futile call to Stephanie's number and he was ready. He let himself out through the tenement in the rear, and walked three blocks, shambling along. He approached a hack line and stepped in the head cab, rousing to life a startled, incredulous driver.

"Calvert Street," he snapped. "On the West Side. In a hurry!"

The cab moved, and he sat back. He felt the cold relief of ultimate decision. A die was cast, and an issue joined. And the night was grim and lonely, and full of dire omen, and the conspiring fates looked down upon the night with the brooding, chill detachment of the everlasting stars.

Ward changed his mind on the way to the West Side, and had the driver halt the cab several blocks short of Calvert Street. He waited till the cab was gone, then resumed the way afoot underneath the El along Greenwich. He stood on the corner of Calvert for a time, very convincingly a homeless, miserable waterfront derelict. He felt a sense of keen eyes watching, though he saw none. He scanned the gutters, picked up a dead, half-smoked cigarette, and striking a match, lighted it again. Puffing on the bitter thing, he slowly walked down Calvert Street.

The neighborhood, to outward appearance, was deserted. No one was on the street. He glanced without expression at the doorway where Jessie Wilson once stood of nights. It was empty. He went on.

Garry's, he saw as he passed by, was only moderately crowded, Garry stood at the end of the bar as usual, a chuckle ever ready in his barrel chest, a cigar rolling in his capacious mouth. A swift survey disclosed to Ward no one he could suspect of allegiance to The Eel. He took little assurance from that.

10

PREDICAMENT

WARD STROLLED AROUND the block. He studied the dark, silent houses in the row immediately behind Duff Garry's. They looked all alike, although both lofts and tenements occupied this block. He stood in the shelter of a doorway for a few minutes, brooding, somnolent in appearance. Then he tried the door. It opened on darkness. He entered, struck a match. He was in a malodorous hallway; a rickety stairs led above. He walked to the rear. Another flight of steps led down to a cellar. He went down.

The cellar was a place of piled up refuse and individual padlocked coal bins, and back beyond these things there was a door. Ward made for it. He found himself in a small yard. He moved quickly, locating a door in the fence at the rear. It let him into the little patch of yard attached to Duff Garry's place, recognizable by the light in the barred windows and the sound of glasses and men's voices in the open air shaft between buildings.

Ward waited in the yard for a time, allowing his eyes to accustom themselves fully to the semi-darkness and to identify every unknown shadow.

Thought was quickened in him, spurred by the drama, the rashness of this moment, and he looked with detachment upon himself, and sardonically wondered. He was here of his own volition, and would be nowhere else, and yet his presence here resulted from no desire or plan or reckless conception of his own. A fate was in the saddle; riding hard. Vast forces drove him, whether or no, and he went, willingly driven, although with wonder and a loneliness and a bitterness.

He smiled at himself, a little crookedly, acid-humored. One thing he knew, at least. There was relief in action, catharsis in violence, reward enough for the moment in the brute exaction of vengeance and elemental justice. He advanced to the door, listened, heard nothing but that sound of voices. He took a grip on the butt of the .45, and slowly, tensely, turned the knob.

The door led on an empty, dimly lighted corridor. Ward studied it, recognizing the door opening on the card room where Teverson had kept rendezvous with his seagoing associates. Opposite it another door led somewhere. Beneath the card room door a sliver of light shone; the other was dark.

Ward went silently to the card room, listened, peered through the keyhole. He was unable to see a single face, although half a dozen men occupied the room. They talked earnestly in subdued tones, the words indistinguishable.

Ward swore, stood looking at the door opposite a moment, then drew his gun, turned the knob carefully, and threw the door wide open. The room was dark, unoccupied; there was a cot, a chair, some blankets and clothing. Across the room was a window.

Ward went quickly to the window. It was not barred; it opened on the air shaft. While he looked, a man entered the hallway, strode solidly. Ward sprang without a sound across the room, and stood tensely against the wall just within the door. The door was partly open, and he dared not close it now. Death was a presence in the room.

The man in the hallway paused, grunted, and pulled the door shut smartly. It was Duff Garry. Ward moved, gripped the knob, waited in darkness. Garry opened the door to the card room opposite; the voices were suddenly clearer.

"Come on in, Duff," a hoarse, sardonic voice invited. There was intimate understanding in the tone, but there was also measurable menace. "Maybe you can help us out a bit. We've got a tough citizen to deal with. He doesn't feel like talking."

"You guys are crazy!" Garry said earnestly, desperately. "This ain't no place to do that. Suppose the man on the beat walks in?"

"Keep him out!" someone said flatly.

"Try and do it! Why don't you do this job some place where there can't be any interference? Think of me!"

"THAT'S JUST WHAT I was doing," drawled the sinister voice. "I thought possibly you could promote a general improvement in this guy's memory. He won't talk, and he can't remember. In fact, I can't understand what good he's doing to anybody on this earth at all. Can't you help him out? Come on, Duff—what do you think he ought to remember best? You know him pretty well."

"I told you everything I know," Garry said in a tone of constant reiteration. "I can't read his mind for you."

"You told us he lived at the Blassingame. You said he was smuggling hot ice and such goods. You passed along a lousy tip about the Waldorf-Ritz. All we've got so far is a couple of stiffs and a bunch of cripples, and one haul of stuff on its way off a Greek freighter in Erie Basin." The voice turned into a snarl, lashlike. "That's not enough! I'll burn his feet to the bone to get what I want, and yours too, Garry! I'm going back to Jules with a complete story if I have to tear a couple of tongues out to make sure of it. Dammit, I want talk! Do you hear me, the two of you? *I want talk!*" A table jumped from the force of the blow accompanying the statement.

The small hairs on Ward's neck were stiff, erect, and his blood was hot, hot with fighting rage. He controlled himself. He slowly turned the knob in his hand, opened the door on a slit.

Duff Garry stood in the opposite doorway, apprehensive, suffering. Beyond him the room was full of men. In a far corner sat Teverson.

Teverson was a shocking sight. He sat slumped low in a chair in a state of desperate exhaustion. His clothes were loosened, and his shirt front was in bloody ribbons. His face was dead white, and his eyes were glowing coals. His mouth was grim, and his jaw set like something of cast iron. He was trapped, tortured, with the look of death on him, yet his fanatic will sustained a defiance that all their efforts could not break.

Equally potent a sight in Ward's eyes was that emphatic speaker. It was the man of the scarred face. The others he did not know. They were diverse types, three or four silent, hard-eyed native born, a couple akin to the Corsican.

There was iron in Dex Ward's soul, and from cold it turned to warm, and from hot to molten metal. He pulled out both guns. He opened the door, carefully. He breathed deeply. He stepped silently across, to take a stand behind Duff Garry. They were totally unaware of him until he was there, wraithlike, looking at them grimly over Garry's shoulder. They were instantly aware of the guns. It was a stunning, flawless coup.

"Don't move, don't stir a hand!" Ward ordered in clipped, hot tones. "Look straight ahead, every one of you. *Straight ahead!*"

Their dazed eyes swung away from him. They sat frozen, transfixed and full of sudden fear. Across the room Teverson came to his feet, astounded and baffled, confused by the raffish disguise, and aflame with incredulous hope.

One fellow, as if hypnotized, still stared at Ward, glassy-eyed. Ward looked at him. The man grunted sharply, looked away. They stared at one another like statues. The scar-faced man remained in his original posture, leaning on the table, gazing at the wall in obedience to the command, his swart face gorged, and he cursed softly, over and over. They were aware of that dread presence of death among them, greedy, leering.

DUFF GARRY SAID hoarsely, "Don't shoot! Don't start anything here, friend. This ain't my party. I didn't want this to happen!"

"Shut up, you skunk!" Ward rasped. "I have plenty of reason here to shoot the liver clean out of you!"

Garry's heavy frame sagged. He begged, "Don't start anything, boys. Do whatever he wants. Don't start anything—I'm between your guns!"

The scarface barked, "Shut up!" with menace, and subsided.

Ward snapped, "Teverson—out of there! Don't get in front of them. Come around behind."

Teverson came. There was an evil, fantastic grin on his drawn face. He paused near the door and held out his hand without looking. Ward put the .45 into it.

"Now—you sons of misbegotten carrion!" Teverson spat at the gathering. "Now I'll do a little talking for you."

Low voiced and sharp, Ward commanded, "Easy, Tev! Keep going."

"You want to know how I conduct my operations in the harbor," Teverson went on, ignoring him. "I'll tell you how. By being smarter than anybody else. By stealth and cunning and brains. By paying off on the nail and paying on word alone. By plugging the man that meddles with any man of mine. Do you want to know how many I've personally disposed of in the past two years?"

"Six!" snapped the scarface.

"Correct!" said Teverson. "You got two of mine, but I'm still ahead. And I'll stay ahead. You mugs could never work my racket in a thousand years. You haven't the brains, and no one will ever trust you. You're water rats—chiseling, penny ante thieves. Rats you'll live and rats you'll die!"

"Tev!" Ward snapped. "Come out here!"

Teverson laughed at the gang, a hard, ugly, sneering laugh, paying no attention. He cursed them, with an eloquence of detail that was bloodcurdling, a little sickening, viewing its cause. The man was in the grip of hysteria; the ordeal he had passed through, and the reserve of strength and will he had depleted, left him unstrung, almost homicidally unbalanced.

Ward shoved Garry quickly out of the way, and reached

in and took Teverson's elbow. He jerked Teverson bodily out from the room. There was fear in Ward that the .45 would presently begin to deal out bloody execution, and that a shambles would come. They must escape while this spell was on the gang.

"Go in that room across," Ward ordered desperately. "There's a topcoat there, and a hat. Put them on, and cover up."

Teverson, all at once silent, submissive, obeyed. Ward remained in the card room doorway, watching the gang. There was reluctance in him, a grim, fierce reluctance.

"I'm going to close this door," he told them. "Nothing will happen—now! You're going to stay right where you are for some time. Teverson is going to get a cab and get clear of the neighborhood, and I'm staying here to see that he has all the time he needs. If you doubt me—step out and stop a bullet! You with the scar! Do you understand me?"

"I get it," the man said venomously.

Ward drew the door partly to, reached to its inner side and withdrew a key from the lock. He closed the door and locked it from the outside. Teverson was in the doorway opposite, leaning against the door jamb.

"Come on, Tev," Ward snapped. "Let's get out of here."

THEY WALKED THROUGH the barroom and out of the place. Their chins were in their coat collars, their hats low on their eyes. A few glanced at them, but no one paid special attention. Ward steered Teverson to the left, to West Street. On West Street they walked a few blocks uptown until a flying taxicab made an abrupt stop at Ward's whistled summons. They climbed in. The cab moved off.

Teverson lay back in the seat, eyes closed. Ward looked at him, took his wrist and felt the pulse. "Tev! How goes it?"

The response was delayed, "All right, I suppose."

"What did they do to you?"

"They used knives. Two of them held me. Another slashed me."

Ward uttered an oath, softly. "Bad?"

"Not yet. They hadn't come to that. Did you ever hear of the Chinese torture they call the Death of a Thousand Cuts?"

"I have."

"I know all about it. I think I've lost a lot of blood. It's trickled into my shoes."

"I'll have a look at you soon as we get home."

They rode the rest of the way in silence. Ward's thoughts were tense and a little bleak. The thought of Jules Koerner, The Eel, was a crushing thing.

The man, his methods and his gang, loomed like a doom in the night, entirely too overpowering to combat.

Reaction had Teverson so weak that Ward had to support him into the South Street house. Ward got him to his bed, and swiftly removed his clothes. The sight of Teverson's naked form shocked him even now. He brought a basin of warm water, cotton and medicaments, and cared for the wounds. None was deep or, barring infection, serious of itself. It was their calculated number, their fiendish cumulative effect, that told on a victim.

Ward had considered the possible need of medical attention, the contingency of blood transfusion, but when he was done dressing the lacerations, he decided against doing more tonight. It would be impossible to give adequate explanation of this to a suspicious medico, and a report to the police must be avoided at any cost.

Teverson fell into deep sleep, and Ward, with the side lamp dimmed by a scarf, sat beside the bed without moving for a long time, watching him. Outside, the sounds of the city were like the breathing of a limitless monster, a distant roaring, rising and falling, never ceasing. Occasionally, as if in troubled dreams, the monster stirred, and a deep-toned harbor whistle hoarsely moaned its massive plaint, over the dark waters and over the city.

Ward thought of the years, the glittering years, and of this man, of whom the memory of those years was forever full, and by whom it was forever colored in such vivid hues. They had been friends, they had shared without stint, of pleasure and pain alike.

And how little known they were to one another in the end! Ward thought, how blind and lonely an animal is man, and how, in his rebellion against that doom, he joys in giving hurt, delights to fight, to maim and kill. This man he nursed so anxiously now—they had fought, and fought again, and they would fight still more, and neither wish nor will nor clearest vision of that fateful destiny could abate it by one jot.

The telephone called him from the bedside. It was Stephanie. She had been calling the past hour. She wished to see him, she had important information.

"Will it keep till tomorrow?" he asked. "I can't leave here now."

"You cannot? Why not?"

"Teverson's been hurt. They got their hands on him

tonight. I barely got him away. I want to stand by till I'm sure he's all right."

Alarm quivered in her voice. "Oh, what have they done? Tell me, Dex. Don't put me off, please."

HE TOLD HER the details curtly. "I'm sure it was stopped in time. He's in a state of exhaustion now. The shock was severe, as it was intended to be. Don't worry about him. I'm taking good care, and I'll call you in the morning."

"Do call me. Early."

"And what's this information you have, Stephanie?"

"It is about that girl. Jessie Wilson, It is no use telling you all this now. I wish to see you tomorrow."

"Hm." Ward paused. "Look here. Why not come over here tonight? We can put you up. And perhaps you can help nurse the patient."

He could almost hear her think. Then she said slowly, "No, I think not, Dex. It is not the best thing."

"Why not?"

"You are slow to understand."

Perhaps he was. And perhaps not. His jaw set, and his nostrils flared a little in sudden anger. He controlled his tone.

"Very well, Stephanie. We'll get together tomorrow. I'm closing all deals in the morning. I'll have the stuff expressed to New York and held for shipment at any moment. I'll let you know how things go."

He was quick to hang up.

Thereafter he paced the larger room, subduing the devil that raged in him. It was a devil he disavowed, but it would not depart. It was a devil of passion and hatred. Hatred of the man who lay in the other room. Hatred of the woman who could rouse him, who did rouse him, wishing something from him, beguiling him. And who drew back, intimating other loyalty, other ownership. Because Teverson was prostrate, and he, Dex Ward, was not, because a devil was in him and she knew it, she shrank from coming.

And then Ward abruptly sat down and pressed his temples between his hands and groaned a little, and he was glad that she had decided so. It was, quite as she maintained, not the best thing. A thing that Teverson once had said now bound him, a lonely phrase isolated in the midst of all his high circumstance and arrogance, a plea of deepest need. He had said—I need a friend. And so it was and would be.

In the morning, Teverson was recovered to a marked degree. He got up, and ate a hearty breakfast. A layer of dressing and bandage shielded his wounds from painful contact with clothing. He lay down afterwards again and read the newspaper. Ward permitted him to rest until midmorning, when he felt quite satisfied with the patient's condition and prepared to go uptown on the gun deal.

"Tev, do you feel fit enough to tell me more about last night?" he asked.

Teverson reflected, somberly. "There isn't much to tell. I was fed up with this place. I'm not accustomed to inaction, to hiding. I phoned Inspector Dineen and wrangled with him for a while. He tried to honey me into taking a pinch as a formality, but I declined. He offered a deal—a private conference, with immunity. I said I'd think it over. I gagged on thinking presently, and grabbed my hat and lit out. Too many loose ends to think about. I made up my mind to chance it over to Duff Garry's. There might be messages, and there would be chance to check up on Captain Carnigan."

"Don't ever tell me I'm a damned fool again!" Ward growled.

"I SEEM TO have lost the privilege. I walked in. Garry looked flustered, but hearty as ever. We decided it would be best to have our talk in the back room. We were there about twenty minutes when the door opened, and that gang trooped in, guns drawn. They chased Garry out. I got the drift of things instantly. Garry has double-crossed us. Somebody there phoned The Eel gang that I'd shown up. Garry's responsible for that raid on the Blassingame and for Ali's death."

"And possibly for our first unpleasantness at his place. I've been doing a little thinking myself. He sent you out into that crossfire of guns. Why didn't he accompany us? Or let us out a back way?"

"I've thought of that," Teverson said wearily. He was silent a moment, then said, "You may understand now, Dex."

"Understand what?"

"Why I didn't let you into my confidence. Why the racket remained a mystery. I didn't want you to know. I saw it becoming too terrible a responsibility to wish you to share it. If you ever fell into their hands...."

"Well?" dryly. "You'd come get me out, wouldn't you?"

"If I knew where you were!" Teverson snorted, suddenly roused. "Look here. How in hell did you come to barge in there last night? I barely recognized you. I doubt that any of that gang knew you."

"The course was plainly indicated. Duff Garry had

already crossed me. It was logical he'd do the same to you. I put on the false-face so no one would stop me on the way."

"Crossed you? How?"

Ward told him of the ambush at the Waldorf-Ritz, and of his escape. He left out any mention of Dr. Beecher.

Teverson swore. "Well, this wipes Duff Garry out completely. And leaves Carnigan up in the air. But I can see how it came about. Garry's a law-abiding citizen now, licensed and paying taxes. Once he was a dangerous man to cross. Now he's disarmed, helpless, chained to one spot where his investment is, and at the mercy of anyone walking in with a gun."

"The sentiment is truly Christian and commendable," Ward drawled with a flash of steel in the tone. "But it doesn't solve the problem. What are you going to do about him?"

Teverson was silent. "I don't know."

"What was this you once asked me about people who have designs on your life? About shooting in cold blood?"

Teverson groaned, and turned face to the wall. "Go sell your papers," he said. He covered his head with the bedclothes, and was still. He did not speak or stir again while Ward was in the house.

11

A VISIT FROM SPIDER

THE VARIOUS TRANSACTIONS necessary for the assembly of the war materials in the Port of New York, ready for export shipment, took up most of the remainder of Ward's day. They were almost purely routine, as all preliminaries had been covered and since Ward had sufficient money to make initial payments in cash on everything. Sevier agreed to procure the export license from the Federal Munitions Control Board, a necessary but simple formality.

That noontime brought an unexpected and valuable encounter. Ward was waiting in the lobby of the Hotel Shentland for Macdonald Sevier, glancing over a newspaper, when a stout, dark little man with a waxed mustache seated himself alongside, and leaning close, said quietly, "I am of infinite relief to see you. I have had the distraction."

Tensing a little, Ward said noncommittally, "Really now?"

"I do not know your name," the man went on. "But you are acquainted to me from the Hotel Blassingame. I know that you are associated to Mr. Teverson and I may speak. Is it that one may know where is Mr. Teverson? For two days I cannot find him."

Ward sized up the man. He looked familiar. And then

the quaint, precisely distorted English clicked in his recollection. He was one of those who came for secret conferences with Teverson.

"Hasn't Teverson sent you any message?"

"I have no message. I read of the murder in the hotel apartment, and I am lost to think, I have the distraction. But all marches well, no?"

"Fairly well. Teverson had an accident, and is laid up a few days. He prefers to keep his whereabouts to himself. I'll be glad to give him any message."

The man fussed a little within himself, like a kettle boiling impatiently. "I wish to make some business immediately. It is not possible to delay. Today I must cable friends in Barcelona. It is a desperation."

"Let's have it then. Perhaps I can help you out."

The matter, Ward inferred from the man's description, was a typical Teverson case. A family in Castile was secretly preparing for flight to the sanctuary of a foreign land, before participation by the clan in an abortive revolutionary conspiracy was unearthed by the vengeful government in power. Their home and lands must be abandoned, for they dared not offer the properties for public sale. They had in their possession, however, a large sum of bank notes and gold, and the jewelry of three generations of beautiful women. They would be subjected to search, crossing the border, and their wealth confiscated, if they tried to take it with them. They were torn between the prospect of courts martial and military execution on one hand, and impoverishment in exile on the other.

Then an experienced friend informed them of Teverson's good offices. They made frantic contact with an agent in Barcelona. The agent, apprised by Teverson's cable of the suspension of all activity, put them off, but promised to see what could be done. He was unable to reach Teverson, but managed to state the case to the stout little gentleman—Señor Rondalvo, by his own declaration—who in turn promised to make earnest search for Señor Teverson. Without Señor Teverson, who knew so well the what-you-call, ropes, the project was impossible. Would the good Señor Teverson agree to make the exception and help these miserable unfortunates?

Ward was dubious. "I don't see how he can manage it, Señor Rondalvo."

"But there is, I am told, a ship in the harbor of Barcelona which proceeds tomorrow. It is a ship with agents most to be trusted, men of the crew. This family must act within forty-eight hours. The fortune of this family can be transported secretly aboard within one hour. This minute can I send a cable—if I am of assurance that there is the cooperation of Señor Teverson."

Ward weighed the matter. It swept him along a bit, the very appeal of adventure in it uprooted his misgivings and objections. He said abruptly, "Send your cable. Tell them to go ahead. I'll see it's taken care of at this end, in the usual manner, and at the customary terms."

The little man sputtered effervescent gratitude and lifelong indebtedness. Ward, cutting it short, demanded details of the ship at Barcelona. It was the S.S. *Caliban*, Jonathan Short, Master, out of Erie Basin on the Mediterranean run. It was due home in eleven days. Rondalvo had his information precisely in mind, and Ward gained a clear picture of the technique involved.

FOR AN INSTANT, Ward wondered why, if this fellow knew so much, he did not assume the responsibility and the task himself, and in consequence, the profits. But the answer came quickly. There was more required than mere knowledge; there was the faculty, the talent for the iron rule of reckless men, for fending trouble, for anticipating danger and meeting it more than half way. Ward's esteem for Teverson's accomplishments was raised considerably. Teverson had become what he was because he'd had what it takes!

In parting, Rondalvo presented his card, scribbling his telephone number on the back. He exacted a promise that Ward would relieve his mind of any lingering doubt by telephoning assurance that Teverson had endorsed Ward's decision. He went bouncing off in high self-satisfaction.

IN MID AFTERNOON, Ward dropped into the office of H. Holtz, Inc., on 42nd Street, to salute the bored looking brunette beauty holding down the outer desk and walk directly into the boss's private office.

"So! It's you," Hymie greeted him. "I got the dope two hours already. I'm ashamed to take your money."

"Why, I wouldn't embarrass you for the world, Hymie!" Ward protested. "Just say the word, and I'll tear it up."

"No, no! Don't bother. I can stand it. Here is the report McGuire telephoned in." He handed Ward the typed document.

It was a little masterpiece. The subject's name was Angelo Bellini. Born, Sardinia. Age 26. Arrived U.S. age six months. Father, Mike Bellini, naturalized citizen, proprietor Bellini, Inc., gravestone and monument works,

*Ward was aflame
with killing fury*

Throgg's Neck, East Bronx, New York. Subject bred to the trade, but only occasionally working at it, due to slack times last few years. Played violin in amateur dance orchestra, apparently making contacts which drew him increasingly away from home and home neighborhood. Said to be well supplied with money, presumably through musical engagements, but, in the opinion of certain disapproving neighbors, more likely through unnamed but rumored lawless activity.

There was much more. The important item among a great deal of irrelevant details was the statement that the subject was reported to spend at least one day at home each week.

"Listen, Hymie. Put a man up there and watch for this fellow. I want to know when he's there. By the report, it'll only be a few days at most."

"I should care how many days! I'll put a man."

"I'll call this office at regular intervals to get the reports. I have another job also. I want you to find a sea captain for me. A Captain Carnigan, master and owner of the freighter *Campeche,* home port New York. I have no idea where he is, and don't care to go asking myself."

"Okay. Such a man I could find over the telephone without leaving the office."

"Find him. Talk to him if possible. Tell him this. That a certain party, with whom he has done a great deal of business of a private nature in the past, wishes very much to get in touch. Get his telephone number or address. Tell him there's a good charter and a fat profit involved."

Hm," ruminated Hymie, studying Ward. "Bonds! He's selling bonds, is it? He needs a ship now, private chartered, to deliver them, I suppose."

Ward laughed, and let it stand.

It was coming dark when Ward returned to the hideout. No light was lit, and he found Teverson's bed empty. He swore in exasperation and alarm. The man was out of his head to venture forth in his condition!

WARD CALLED STEPHANIE on the telephone, learned that Teverson was not with her, that she had not heard from him at all. He soothed her anxiety, assured her that everything was quite all right. He outlined all he had done that day, to her intense gratification. Plans were progressing.

"How about meeting me sometime tonight, Stephanie?" he concluded. "I want very much to hear what you've learned about Jessie Wilson,"

"I will come over. I prefer not to come to your place."

"We can meet outside. Will you come over in the boat?"

"If you say."

"Head in for shore at Corlear's Hook. There's a park there. I'll watch for you."

"If you will have a small flashlight and answer my signal, I will pick you up quickly. Ten o'clock is all right?"

"Ten it is."

He had barely hung up when Teverson came in. He looked all in, and sank into a deep chair.

"Where in hell did you take yourself on a day like this?" Ward demanded.

Teverson pulled a number of bulky envelopes from various pockets, tossing them on a table. "Make me a drink, Dex. I've been on plenty business."

Ward glanced into the envelopes. They were all stuffed with money in large bills. He got the drink before inquiring further.

"What's all the cash for?"

"I collected all I could. I cashed in everything I could draw on."

"But what are you going to do with it?"

Teverson looked at him. Something like hatred fired in his gaze. "None of your damned business! Who's running my affairs, you or I?"

Ward shrugged and walked away. He went in the kitchen, pried open several tins of food, and threw together a warm and savory, if sketchy meal. They ate with spasmodic and monosyllabic conversation.

"How's the chest?"

"Coming along."

"Hurt?"

"A little."

"I'll change the dressing."

"Never mind. Did it myself."

Then silence. The tension of it was not pleasant.

Ward thought it over carefully while clearing up, and decided to lay before Teverson the deal he had made with Señor Rondalvo. Teverson listened without expression, and then said tersely, "Can't touch it. You had no right to make such an agreement."

"Well, I did," Ward asserted flatly. "So what are you going to do about it, and why can't you touch it?"

"You ask *why!* After these days and weeks. Two of my men knifed to death to your own knowledge, and probably others murdered I haven't yet heard about. My apartment wrecked, my whole racket stripped and exposed, myself put through the mill last night. Everything shot to pieces, and both of us driven to hide in this hole for fear of our lives. Dammit, you don't use your head, you don't realize I The Eel and his mob have my number, and in my best day I was only able to operate because they couldn't figure out what was going on."

WARD STARED AT him. "Tev, aren't you going to fight it out?"

"Fight what? Who? Show me where to begin!"

Ward took a deep breath. "All right. Skip that. But let's make a deal. Let me handle this."

Teverson's eyes narrowed. "You actually want to?"

"I've got to. I made a promise, and I can't let those people down."

Teverson grunted, studied a fingernail. "Well… have it your way. I still won't touch it. Do a job, and if you live, take a cut of the commission." He added grimly, "I'm not responsible."

At ten o'clock Ward walked along the river walk at Corlear's Hook, one eye on the river and another, warily, on the strollers in the park. A powerful, muted throbbing came out of the night, and Stephanie's boat approached with a great thrust of white water from the bows. It passed, and a tiny light winked. Ward answered. The craft cut about and came back, coasting, drawing carefully inshore.

When Ward sprang into the cockpit, the man at the wheel headed the boat northward again and let her out to full speed. The deep baying of the exhaust and the mighty wash of the waters prevented any exchange of words with Stephanie until he had settled close to her, leaning back on the leather cushions, shoulders touching. Her eyes glinted with a light like the sheen of radiance on the dark rippling tide, and the perfume of her was heady in his nostrils.

She shouted, barely audible, "Do not talk yet. We speed for precaution. Later."

They sat together, wordless. They sped beneath the enormous Williamsburg Bridge. In the night on either side the soaring towers of the city glimmered, like jet studded with brilliants. Ahead, looming swiftly, Welfare Island lay in the river, a miniature Manhattan straddled by the great Queensborough span. They streaked past a glowing Long Island Sound steamer, and headed for the treacherous cross-rips of Hell Gate.

The speed did not abate until they had reached the spacious dark and quiet of the Sound. Then Stephanie's man nosed the craft in gently toward land. He found a small dock by starlight and tied up. The land here came to a point, and beyond the scant beach reared a black, unrecognizable mass of masonry. Making no inquiry, Ward studied it, and suddenly knew where he was.

It was old Fort Schuyler, obsolescent and abandoned, grass grown and brooding with memories of vanished glory.

They climbed to the top of the rampart, where they sat on the turf in the cool starlight.

"I find this two months ago," Stephanie told him, "and I come here when I wish to have peace for a little. There are not many places I may go, and forget. It is rash to come with you, I think, Dex Ward, but all of a sudden for once I do not care."

He tore bits of grass from the ground, slowly. "You needn't be afraid of me, Stephanie. I know damned well where I stand!"

"Oh… it's not you. Not you I fear."

He was perfectly still. "Who then?"

"You do not understand yet? It is myself."

A silence. "Why?"

"I am so alone, Dex. For months I have been all alone,

and there is danger and strain, and I have no one to turn to. And I fear to trust my impulse and my judgment, for I am not a normal woman this way."

"Stephanie," he said, "they address you as 'Madame.' You're married?"

"No, I am not. It is because I travel alone that I am 'Madame.' And Gorda is of course an adopted name."

"And Teverson?"

"What of Teverson? A man whose help I needed, who is half-fascinated and jealous, and at the same time deathly afraid of me. Oh, you are so foolish, Dex Ward."

HE STARED AT her in the faint, unreal light, his blood pounding. "Stephanie…!"

And all at once she was in his arms, and he held her, powerfully, and she did not speak, but was crying, with relief, with escape from strain and tension, with surrender to the fact that she was a woman, and too much alone.

They talked then, of things remote from Teverson, and The Eel, and the tragedy of Berengaria. There was an overtone of desperation in Stephanie's voice, as if she stood on the verge of the deep end, poised there, torturing herself, knowing she must turn back, go back.

"Dex, I am wrong, I am evil, to let this happen!"

"Wrong? To acknowledge something bigger than either of us, Stephanie?"

"It is weakness to admit there is anything bigger."

"Not to my way of thinking."

"Oh yes, it is so—*for us*. I would not come to you last night because I fear to be alone with you. I should *want* too much to admit that. I could not play the coquette. And it is vain and impossible that we should… should come to love each other."

"Tell me why it's impossible, Stephanie."

"We are not people fit for love or for each other. We have much to do, all too much. You must know that I cannot be with you, that I must soon go."

"Home?"

"But certainly, without choice or alternative, Dex. I must go to my father and my people, and be with them in the great trial that is coming. It is my duty. My mission is almost now done."

He did not speak for a moment. "When must you go?"

"I go… on this ship with the planes and munitions."

He tried to shut off the crowding, clamoring future, to hide from it and not gaze into its hollow face, but he could not do it.

"Stephanie," he cried suddenly, desperately, "you've done your duty and run all the risk your country could ask. You are not a soldier like your father, to give a lifetime and dedicate a career. You are a woman, with a woman's life to live. You're not a strong young man, to go back and bear arms into battle."

"Oh, but I am!" she declared with a trace of mystic exaltation. "You don't know the women of my country. In the hills, they have fought beside their men for a thousand years, defending the passes, resisting invasion in their homes, dying in battle if so God wills! You think I can hide while they go to fight?"

"You think your father will allow you to court more danger after this mission of yours? After dodging assassins' bullets and hiding in daily fear of your life?"

"I am my father's son and daughter both, and where he goes, I go. Until he falls, I shall follow him. There is no other way."

And then, as the enormity of what she was saying was suddenly clear to her, she clung to him convulsively. "Oh, what will I do, Dex? I did not want this. I am not of my right mind. But, Dex… oh, what will I do without you?"

HE SOUGHT, TORMENTED, for comfort to give her. She accepted what little he could offer, craved it, even though it was vain. The moment passed. She gradually calmed, drained both of dread and passion.

She got up abruptly, shivering. The urge to flight was in her. She could not remain in this place of pain and desperation any longer. She led the way back to the boat, and he followed perforce. They were both cold, as if the chill of the dark waters was especially piercing tonight. They climbed in, and she ordered that they proceed back to the East River again, running slowly.

"Now it is necessary that we talk of other things, Dex Ward," she told him evenly. "I will tell you what I have found about the death of Jessie Wilson."

He growled, "Go ahead."

"I have found who is the murderer. He is a man they call 'Spider.' His real name is Martin Webb, and he is a bad man, so it was natural that they call him 'Spider Webb,' I suppose. He is one of the men who is with this man, The Eel. He is a man of your age, very dark and unpleasant of appearance, and there is a bad razor scar on his face. That is what I am told."

He was struck. "How did you learn this, Stephanie? That's the very man!"

"I was so concerned for you. You were in too great danger to go find anything there for yourself. I thought, what could I do that you could not do? And suddenly I knew. You could not go and ask questions as a woman could go. Many languages from my part of Europe I speak, some very well, some enough to talk with simple people. I could perhaps do something that no one else could do for you."

"You went to that house?"

"I went there. Early in the day, when the women of the neighborhood were at home and the men away and the least danger to be met there. I knocked on doors and said I wrote pieces for the newspaper and I wished to write about the poor girl who was dead. Some of them slammed the doors in my face, and some talked and said nothing but words—and then a little old woman who lives right across the landing from this Jessie Wilson, she told me the whole story! She, who has no family, no friends, but far away in the old country, wept when I spoke an old country greeting, and she told me the story in her native tongue."

"Will she tell it to the police?"

"She would not when I first spoke, but she will now. You know why?"

HE SMILED A little, grimly. "I can imagine anybody telling anything after you talked to them a while, Stephanie."

"I should not say this, but that you must understand. I told her that you were to be punished unjustly for the crime. And I told her that I loved you."

A silence, and then he said huskily, "Go on."

"You remember when you walked from the door of this Jessie Wilson? You have told that you felt as if eyes watched you, hating you? You were not wrong. This old woman, crooked like a little bent stick with age, and living alone, sits many evenings in her room with the door opened only a very little, sitting there in darkness, rocking her old body and looking at all who pass, and hating most of them for her loneliness. She saw you enter, and she hated you. For the girl she prayed and was pitying. She saw you go out again, and watched you with only greater hatred. She did not know then; did not know until I told her the reason why you were there."

"She might have liked me even less. I was indirectly responsible for that killing."

"But you wished the girl well, and it is the evil in the heart of that other that is responsible. This little old woman, she saw in a little while the man Spider come to the girl's door. The girl tried to send him away without opening the door, but he made such insistence that she let him in. Their voices sounded through the door, low but very angry. There was, my old woman thinks, a blow or a scuffle. Then there was a long silence, and this Spider comes out quietly and goes quickly away. My old woman sits there, thinking with pity of the girl and with hatred for all the men, and much time passes. And then is the smell of gas, and a great fear comes to my old woman. She goes to the janitor of the building, and finally makes him understand, and they call the police in much alarm. The police come—and you know what they find."

"Hm! How is it the old woman didn't tell the cops all this?"

"Once she tried to, but they are busy and they laugh at her poor speech, which is hard to understand in English, and they decide she is what you say, cracked in the head a little. And she, hating the men, hates them too, and she closes her mouth and tells nothing more."

"And now she'll talk, eh?"

"She will, because she says she believes now that you had good in your heart—and because she would help the lover of the young girl who came to her with words of greeting in her own tongue."

And so ended that unhappy evening together. They discussed business and finances, but Stephanie withdrew into some remoter inner self, and Dex Ward was baffled and could not follow. He read her wish to be gone in the austerity of her new mood.

12

MYSTERY SCHOONER

HE LEFT THE boat at a slip south of Corlear's Hook. He watched broodingly while the racing craft bore her away with a final wave of the hand. He breathed a deep breath, and headed home.

Teverson was at the piano. He merely glanced up, expressionless, without saying a word, and continued to play. He looked a little pale, but much stronger. Ward, not recognizing the music, but responding to its slow grandeur and melancholy enchantment, stole a look at the sheet music on the rack. It was Grieg's *Concerto in A Minor.* Then he remembered it; Tev played now from the second movement. He sat down to listen.

He did not sit still long. This movement, plaintive, touched with ineffable sadness and resignation, worked like acid on raw nerves. It was utterly out of tune with the moment, with both their lives. It was an evil omen.

Ward got up and picked up the telephone and stepped into the kitchen, closing the door on the cord. He called Hymie Holtz's penthouse.

"Sure, I got it already," said Hymie. "This Captain Carnigan, he's in town, and he was excited to hear what you said to tell him. His ship he's got over in Hoboken, repairing, waiting for cargo, he says. He seemed to know who was inquiring for him, even though I gave no names."

"Where can I find him?"

"He said he is staying in Hoboken, but tonight he will be all evening at a place… Wait, I have the address here. It's Duff Garry's. On Calvert Street, downtown. You know it?"

Ward's lips curled, forming an oath, in chagrin and cynical acceptance. "Yes, I know it. I'll get in touch. Good work, Hymie! You'll hear from me."

He thought that over for a while, swearing at his luck, wondering how to tackle this problem. He made up his mind and went to work preparing his ragged derelict disguise.

Within the hour, Ward shambled past Duff Garry's tavern, peering in with the bleak look of a man shut out. There was a fair crowd tonight. At the bar a convivial, hearty group of men was gathered, most any one of whom might be Carnigan. Ward went on, shivering a little in his scant apparel.

A few blocks from Calvert on the Hudson shore, he entered a ferry house and made a telephone call from a booth. He called Garry's number, and asked if Captain Carnigan were in the house, and if so, to put him on.

A short wait, and a booming voice responded. It was the captain.

Ward said tersely, "Carnigan, listen carefully. I'm talking for Teverson. I want to see you. I can't go into Garry's for the best of reasons. I have a ripe job for you, and want you to come out and meet me. But don't utter a word about the job, about Teverson, or about me. Garry hasn't told you we've been looking for you, has he?"

"I see," said the captain, playing up. "Not a damned word! Yes, I see. Go on."

"Garry's doublecrossing us, Carnigan. I'll line it all up for you later. Say one of your A.B.'s called you from a police station—anything—but get a move on and hop a cab and meet me, say, at Spring and Broadway in fifteen minutes."

"You motherless ape!" said Carnigan, with startling irrelevance. "A hundred dollars' bail? I've a mind— Well, all right. I'll be there in fifteen minutes." And he hung up.

Ward smiled dryly, replacing the receiver. Captain Carnigan sounded interesting.

Captain Carnigan was interesting. He was a giant of a man with a rolling stride almost too salty to be true. He filled the door of the taxi as he climbed out; and startled pedestrians turned to look as he roaringly hazed the driver, apparently out of habit, while paying him off.

Ward shuffled up to the big man.

"Carnigan—you're alone?"

It was Carnigan's turn to be startled. He stared at the unkempt object accosting him. "Who the hell are you? Certainly I'm alone, if it's any of your damned business!"

Ward straightened up, grinned. "It is. My name's Ward. I'm here for Teverson. Overlook the appearance. It has a purpose. Let's walk over to the Bowery, where I can drink with you without running risk of being thrown out."

A bit bewildered, the captain went along. Ward explained the peculiar circumstances, the rendezvous of last night, and what came of it. Carnigan flashed an occasional look at him as he listened, and the big heavy face grew dour. He swore luridly.

"The dirty scut! I'd like now to pay Duff Garry a visit with my bully boys and wreck the bloody place for him."

"He doesn't matter enough, Carnigan. The Eel is the lad I want. But that's another story, another day. I have different work for you, if you'll take it."

OVER A SCOTCH and soda at a Bowery bar they threshed out the matter of Stephanie's shipment of arms. Carnigan gave no sign of his reaction to the proposal until he had fixed every detail in mind, asking countless shrewd questions, pinning the money and expense down to definite sums, and reviewing realistically every hazard involved. He was a good business man as well as ship's master. He had to be, these days, to make a tramp freighter pay.

Frowning into his glass, he said, "It's a crazy, mad venture. But I've done crazier in my day, and I'll do madder again, I guess. The money is good. I like the side I'll be on in this fight. I'm your man. We'll drink on that."

The details were readily arranged. The materials were being assembled in Brooklyn. The *Campeche* would be prepared to come to her berth at a moment's notice, to load and be gone. Within a few days she'd be on the sea.

"If I didn't have to keep an eye on the bloody ship," said Carnigan, "I'd go along in one of these planes and get into that fight. Man, it sounds like a good one!"

"It'll be a desperate one, but they're confident of taking the present government by surprise. You'll have to see to it that your men don't know anything, or if they do, don't talk."

"They're not loose in the tongue, that crew of mine. I'll guarantee to see the stuff overside without a soul in all Europe knowing."

"Good! Are you going back to Garry's now?"

"I'd better. They think I'm only gone on an errand of mercy."

"Then do this for me. I'll give you time to get back. Then I'll phone you there. I'll want an answer, yes or no, to a question. I want to know if you see in the place a man about my age, dark complected, with a deep scar parting his eyebrow and creasing his nose."

Carnigan snorted. "I saw the fellow before I left. He'd just come in. He looked like a bucko, the kind I take glee in taking down, Is there anything I can do to him?"

Ward laughed shortly." Thanks, no. I'll want only to know if he's there. I can handle the rest myself."

The Spider was still there, by Captain Carnigan's veiled word when Ward called him at Garry's. The Spider was still there when Ward ambled by the tavern a little later. Spider Webb stood sidewise at the corner of the bar, his back to the wall, and he watched the place and he watched the street, and he listened, and he sipped a whisky and occasionally scowled.

Ward crossed the street and seated himself on a low stoop in deep shadow and waited, watching Garry's place. It was a cold vigil, but there was a hard, hot look in his steady eyes. Garry was not in evidence tonight. That, perhaps, was why the Spider lingered, hoping to catch him venturing to show up for a hurried check of the registers. It was quite possible to imagine Spider Webb in bad odor today with his master, and in an ugly frame of mind in consequence.

Ward waited patiently, grimly, for a full hour. The Spider took no second drink, but waxed more and more restive and irritable. He could stand it no longer, evidently, for, with a final glance at the bar clock, he spun a coin across the bar, and walked out of the place. For an instant he stood poised in the doorway, hands deep in side pockets; then he set out toward the river at a brisk pace, breasting the wind that now swept along the riverfront.

Ward was not far behind the Spider, who led the way north on West Street. The great cobblestoned way was quiet at this hour; occasionally an enormous produce truck rumbled to market, infrequently a speeding car swooped, passed, was gone from sight. Spider Webb walked fast, self-absorbed.

THEN THE MAN left the sidewalk and crossed the cobblestones toward the river. Something tightened around Ward's heart. He knew suddenly that here was something of infinitely great significance, that now was to be vouchsafed a first glimpse into mystery hitherto unfathomable. He knew by an instinct more sure and certain than reason.

Spider disappeared momentarily into a mass of parked wagons and trucks just off the river, Ward did not follow directly, but circled, gaining the shadows of the huge pier housing just to the south, and hurrying thence to the mass of vehicles standing where the housing ended. He penetrated among the wagons, grimly on edge with dread of ambush, on edge with fear of losing his quarry.

The docks here were open, lacking the vast enclosing structures rearing in a long line to southward of this point. There was no gate or bar to access to these piers. Passing through the parked mass of wagons, Ward made out the shadowy figure of Spider striding out on the planking of the dock immediately before him. There was no light here but the faint glimmer of the stars, and Ward hurried, silently closing up to the man.

Then all at once Spider vanished. Ward stopped, nonplused, suspicious. He crouched, to silhouette things against the night glow better, to reduce his own visibility. He studied the deep obscurity. And suddenly realized Spider had stepped off the dock. A craft of some kind was moored alongside, a craft with masts. He approached, stealthy as a shadow.

It was a schooner, a three-master, and as far as Ward could make out, a fine, shipshape vessel. Very likely an auxiliary motor lay below decks. He was puzzled, trying to account for the schooner—and for Spider's errand aboard.

The saloon lights amidships were faintly aglow with shaded light. Ward watched the deck, studied every inch of it. He saw no sign of a watchman. He saw nothing stir. The tide, running out, was still high, and the deck not far from the dock level. Ward let himself down to the rail, then to the deck. He waited, then without a sound walked toward the saloon ports.

Suddenly, without reason, a chill formed at the back of Ward's neck, and traveled the length of his spine. He did not alter his slow pace or look around. He thought, lightning fast, striving to account for that phenomenon. There was no sound, no alarm. But there was something. And it was behind him.

He chose his fractional second, and whirling about, crouched low on the deck, the .45 half-drawn, eyes boring into the darkness.

A tall shadow loomed. It had been creeping up on him.

It was a man, and with a snarl of hatred, the man instantly charged.

Ward jerked out the automatic and fired. The shot failed, evidently, for the man was upon him, swinging something—blackjack or loaded hose. Ward did nothing so rash as to back away into the orbit of the weapon; he butted the dark figure, grappled with the man.

Sounds of running and of alarmed, angry shouting came almost immediately from below deck. Ward and the man, nullifying each other's deadly strength, staggered and flailed around the deck, barely keeping their feet, grunting, cursing, murderous. Ward could not flex his wrist and bring the gun to bear; a grip of iron held his right hand to the other's body. A light from below flashed upward into the darkness.

WARD STROVE IN berserk frenzy. His goal was the outer rail. The other, intent on the gun, failed to read his purpose, and gave ground. Ward knew, with a certainty beyond any he had ever known, that he had perhaps a dozen seconds to remain alive on that schooner's deck. He used them for a single, unreasoned objective.

The struggle waxed fierce at the rail. The man abruptly realized Ward's aim, and he shouted in sharp fear. Ward cursed, strained with a final gigantic effort, and got the other against the rail. He sensed suddenly that the man could not swim. He butted the man's face with his head, shoved with crazed strength—and over the rail the man toppled, and over with him in unbreakable hold went Dex Ward. They hit the water with a scream and a great splash.

Ward was aflame with lustful satisfaction, with killing fury. Together they plunged beneath the surface. Ward felt the tug and pull of the swiftly ebbing tide. He relaxed, sank. The man, in mad terror, promptly released all holds, and tried to climb Ward's body, struggled to make for the surface, clawing, kicking.

Ward spun him about before he knew what happened, and got a lock hold from behind on head and body. He clung, desperately, grimly, his brain afire, his lungs swiftly approaching the bursting point for need of air. The man struggled, tore at Ward's arms with frantic finger nails, twisted and contorted his body in terror of death. Ward hung on.

Death was beside him also, and that same terror, the terror of the deep dark silent waters. He hung on. And the seconds passed, and the tide swept steadily to sea.

The man's struggle grew quickly feeble. The water was getting him. It was an agonized eternity. Ward clung with a grip of iron. And then the man went limp, and the fingers clawed and scratched no more. Ward caught a hold on the hair of the man's head, and kicked, fought upward in absolute darkness. Panic touched him, direction was lost. Which way was upward in absolute night?

Then his maddened hand felt the chill surface, and he broke through, to gasp in agonized, desperate breathing, barely able to keep upon the surface, burdened so with clothes and with the dead weight of his enemy. He made out the river and the shore line, the docks and the buildings beyond. He was already a distance from the schooner, where beams of light flashed over the waters in search of the struggling pair. The tide swept them fast.

Ward pulled his limp enemy to the surface, turned on his back, and floated as best he could, sustaining the other.

Both were awash, dangerously imperiled by their sodden clothes. Ward was grimly glad now that he was so scantily clad. He swam with one hand, his feet beating a wash of furious white water. He headed toward shore.

It was a veritable grappling with death. Grimly he clung to the leaden body of his enemy, grimly he refused to give it up. They were swept past great shadowy piers where liners docked, unable to reach for their support. They traveled swiftly, pausing now and again to spin in a swirling eddy. But Ward fought the water as he had fought this man, and little by little his unabated energy prevailed. They drew closer to shore.

Then—a pier's end at arm's length! Ward grabbed the man's hair again, rolled over, tore at the water, and caught a hold on the slippery piles. He clung there, the breath sobbing in him, giving thanks to whatever fateful star it was that ruled this night.

13

OUT OF THE RIVER

HE HAULED THE weight of his enemy closer, a little higher out of the water, braced himself, and as a little strength returned, began to look about for a means of getting out of this untenable position to dry land. Clammy cold pierced all his being. The dark waters swirled about, murmuring, cheated and sullen.

After prolonged, cautious exploration, edging along the pier, Ward found a crude ladder nailed to the piles. He maneuvered his limp burden so as to drape the body over his shoulder, and essayed to climb. It was an effort that called upon all his strength; the struggle and the wintry chill had sapped his fierce energy. He gained the top, and rolled over on the pier with his burden. He staggered to his feet, and gave immediate attention to the sodden figure prone beside him.

He grunted. Little examination was needed. The man was apparently quite dead, drowned. Panic had done it. There was no breath, no perceptible heart action. Ward looked about.

He was on another open, empty pier. No vessels were moored here, nobody was around. He dimly made out a fence barring the way from the street. Beyond the fence he saw the lanterns of a street paving job guarding uncompleted work. He ran for the fence.

The gate in the fence was locked to the outside, but inside the lock yielded. Ward ran out on West Street and snatched one of the red lanterns from a stanchion.

One glance at the distorted face of the man on the pier in the eerie red glow from the lantern, and Ward swore with dismay and wrath at the very ironic fate he had blessed a moment before. That face was the last on earth he wished to see in death at this crucial time. It was the scarred face of—Spider Webb!

The man had discovered that he was being followed, then. He had lured his intended victim into a trap. By a freak of circumstance, the trap had snared its maker. And now the killer of Jessie Wilson was forever silenced.

Dex placed the lantern on the planking beside the body, and fled. He ran, to warm himself. A few blocks away, he spied the lighted windows of a tavern not yet closed for the night. He made for it and entered it.

Ward downed two stiff drinks of whisky without pausing. He was stared at, wide-eyed, by an astounded bartender and a pair of customers. Water dripped, forming a pool about his soaked shoes. He stood shivering, waiting for the liquor to warm him. He felt the inner glow begin, and he made for the telephone booth at the rear of the place. He called police headquarters.

Crisply, matter-of-factly, Ward imparted the information that the police might find a drowned man, probably dead, but perhaps in a condition to respond to expert resuscitation, lying on a pier on the Hudson River. The professional, emotionless voice on the wire shot quick questions at him, with no word wasted. Beyond identifying the location of the body, Ward declined to answer them.

"I'll say this, however," he told the voice. "The man is a criminal. He is the killer who murdered Jessie Wilson on Calvert Street. If you found fingerprints in her place other than the one that was published, compare them with his. And have a talk with the old woman who lives across the hallway from the girl's flat—you'll get the entire story from her."

"I'll have the radio alarm go out in thirty seconds," the voice told him. "A patrol will be on hand inside three minutes, and a pulmotor in three more. You wait right there."

"That's not very much time," Ward drawled, grimly, "but I'll bet you'd be surprised if you knew how much ground I'm going to cover in three minutes. I'll call you up again sometime." And he hung up, and ran.

FIVE BLOCKS UP West Street, Ward luckily flagged a stray roving taxi. He bade the driver continue up along the river. Seated shivering inside, he suddenly realized that he had lost his .45 automatic in the watery struggle. He swore, and then was relieved to find the little .25 still secure in a hip pocket. He was satisfied, on second thought, that the .45 was gone; the loss of the heavy weapon had probably been the deciding factor between sinking and staying afloat.

Passing another waterfront tavern, Ward ordered a halt, and went inside for two more shots of whisky. The wind was from the northeast, and the cold pierced his bones. The internal warmth of the whisky helped. But it hindered a little, too, for he felt a little lightheaded after four such portions in so few minutes.

Ward had the cab finally come to a stop close by the yard of parked wagons lying before the open dock. He ordered the man to wait, and ran into the maze of darkened vehicles. He gained the dock, and studied the open space, shivering. His eyes took a moment to focus—but they told him plainly that no vessel was here, no schooner lay moored.

He ran out on the dock. For a moment he was dumbstruck. It was the same dock. That water below, dark and sinister, was the very water into which he had plunged. He could not be so lightheaded as to have dreamed that ordeal.

Then the simple and bitter answer became clear. They had moved the schooner instantly. They must have doubted that either of the murderous contestants ever reached the surface again; but they took no chances. One man had found the ship; so might a second. They had flown, speeding with all the power of the auxiliary into darkness and the night.

And Ward knew then beyond any doubt, with chagrin and frustrate despair, that for a few precious moments he had been within striking distance of the mysterious evil genius of all this waterfront. It was a conviction of instinct. Jules Koerner, The Eel, had been aboard that vessel.

Ward hurried back to the cab, and ordered the man to make for the East Side with all speed. By the time he gained the shelter of the hide-out, a severe, soul-shaking chill had settled in Ward's body. Once again Teverson was not at home. Ward threw off the soaking garments, downed an additional quantity of liquor, and dived into his bed. The alcohol hit him with a shock, the bed and the room spun around. A premonition told him that already he was a sick man, and that the chill, violent and painful, was

no trifling matter. He was unable to calculate the passage
of time, but he knew he had been all too long exposed to
piercing cold. He pulled the clothes over his head. He went
off on a blackout of the world or its problems.

Dex Ward's memory was never to encompass the following morning, nor the next, nor very much the one after that.
For three days he lay in his bed, unaware, except for rare
fleeting seconds, of the world or its problems or concerns.

All he could remember of that time later were glimpses
as through a violet haze, of an anxious face bending over
him, the face of Stephanie, or again of the long, pondering
gaze of Teverson fixed on him. He was a very sick man,
sunk in an abyss of non-existent time.

IT WAS A toss-up during those three days. Medical aid
was perforce a last resort, and they called none in. Stephanie, in common with so many high-born daughters of her
Spartan nation, had studied nursing, had indeed nursed her
father through just such a crisis. Ward's iron constitution
helped tremendously. He was very sick, he verged a hair's-
breadth from a fatal pneumonia—but he pulled through.
He awakened on the fourth morning with a clear head, a
great weakness, and practically no knowledge whatever of
three eventful days.

"This is Tuesday?" he repeated, when Stephanie informed
him of the date. He was genuinely appalled. "Tuesday?
Stephanie—Good Lord!—get me to the telephone! I have
to call half a dozen people. Mac Sevier. Carnigan. Everybody!"

"Quiet—easy!" she warned him, pushing him down in
the bed. "Everything is taken care of."

"Who took care? They don't know where to find me?"

"But you knew where to find them, and I myself called them, every one. Carnigan and his *Campeche* sailed with the munitions last night. They will steam top speed; Rondalvo has given me an inventory of the things coming on the *Caliban* from Barcelona. Your friend, Mr. Hertz, tells me nothing is doing yet at Throgg's Neck." She laughed, soothing his brow. "He is a very funny man."

He was baffled. This was reassuring news, but altogether mystifying. And somewhere or other, it didn't click, failed to fit the pattern. He required much explanation.

"You were raving, the first day," she told him. "You made yourself imaginary telephone calls over and over. You begged me to call them for you. You told me the numbers and the names and what to say Never were you satisfied, even when I tried to assure you that I had taken care."

"I told you everything?"

"Everything. And you talked so! You talked of drowning, of a man drowning. Your clothes were soaking when Tev found them. You can talk clearly now. You can tell me what happened?"

He had to think a moment; Inconceivable that that gruesome business had occurred so many nights ago! "Where's Tev?"

Teverson came on the run, eager and anxious and relieved at the sight of Ward's clear gaze. He listened, and the girl listened, as Ward told them the stark story of that battle under the waters.

Teverson whistled a little. "So that's it! A movable post of command. The base of operations can be changed every night if necessary. Nothing could be better than a boat, for storing guns on standing off a raid. And nothing could look more innocent. Dex, if you'd only stayed off the schooner and gone for help!"

"Hindsight, Tev. Hindsight."

"Yes, I know. It's a chronic affliction these days." Teverson cracked his knuckles like a man tormented, and walked broodingly out of the room.

Stephanie said, "You will eat something now?"

"I certainly will. Not much, maybe, but I'll do my best."

When she brought him a breakfast tray, there was a queer look on Ward's face. "Stephanie! Dammit, I knew something was wrong! Carnigan and the *Campeche* are gone. And you're still here."

She found it unsurprising. "I can postpone my departure. Why not?"

"Why so?" He paused. "Because of me?"

"Because I have one look at this ship *Campeche* and I do not like it. It is old and dirty."

And that was all he could get out of her. But he cherished his own explanation. It made this lay-up almost worth while.

IT WAS HARD to lie quietly in bed, but Ward had to endure several days of inaction. As soon as he was permitted, he reeled his determined way to the telephone, and called up everybody with whom he had been dealing, to make certain of the state of things. Things were, at the moment, satisfactory all around, even though attended by anxious suspense.

Señor Rondalvo was much relieved to hear of his improvement, for the *Caliban* was approaching New York. Hymie Holtz kept a man on steady watch over the monumental works of Bellini, Inc., in Throgg's Neck, and hoped

Ward would be on his feet and ready when word came that Angelo Bellini had turned up. Ward even called Inspector Dillon at Headquarters, to inquire into the fate of Spider Webb. He declined to identify himself. The inspector, grimly trying to drive a bargain with his informant, admitted only that the man was dead. Beyond that, Ward could get nowhere.

Taking advantage of his status as a tottering convalescent who must be humored, Ward bullied Teverson into long and detailed revelations about his affairs. Teverson apparently withheld nothing; he talked with apathy. He was like a man waiting for something, indifferent to what went on around him, indifferent to the past.

Teverson explained that the *Caliban* was another Erie Basin freighter, that the saloon of one Mike Callahan in downtown Brooklyn was the place of rendezvous for that ship. A certain amount of telephoning would be necessary to establish contact. Once done, a meeting would be arranged, and armed with inventory memorandum, and the payoff cash, Ward would travel to Brooklyn and complete the transaction in a private room back of Callahan's bar.

He explained many things, the disposition of foreign paper and bank notes, of gold, the pitfalls of Federal law and foreign edicts, the extent to which American bankers were free to cooperate, the secret resources of the underworld when all else failed, in the disposal of proscribed money. It was an education, and Ward absorbed it all.

And Teverson, playing the piano afterward, seemed to be turning this over in his mind, improvising muted harmonies and glancing every now and then at Ward with a puzzled expression. He went out a couple of times daily, but evidently did not go far, for he was soon back again. The presence of Stephanie made the house more endurable these days. But there was a sickness in Teverson's soul more severe than the malady from which Dex Ward so rapidly recovered.

One afternoon Hymie Holtz reported success when Ward called. Angelo Bellini had come home, had remained the night, and was now working in his father's yard, plainly for diversion rather than any wages. By the signs, he was in no hurry to depart.

"I'll go right up," said Ward. "Call in your man. I'll let you know if I make contact, and how it turns out."

Stephanie was being efficiently industrious in the kitchen, and she observed his preparations with a small frown creasing her brow. He came into the kitchen and went to the small cupboard where Teverson had laid by a miniature arsenal of weapons. He selected a duplicate of the gun he had lost, slid forth the magazine to make certain it was loaded, cocked the mechanism to examine the chamber. Then he slid the automatic in its shoulder holster.

"What is this at Throgg's Neck?" Stephanie demanded.

"A fellow I've been looking for lives up there."

"Who is he? Why do you go there?"

He looked at her. "I'll tell you all about it tonight. This lad's a very important person—but he associates with certain persons of the highest importance."

"There will be trouble?"

He laughed, shortly. "No, I'm afraid not. I can't be that optimistic… You'll be here, I suppose?"

She hesitated, turned away. "You are well again. Now I should go."

HE WENT TO her instantly, took hold of her arm. "Don't go, Stephanie. We need you. I need you, badly. You can help for this little while that's left."

"Some of my countrymen telephone my place, and they are alarmed that I never answer. I forbid my servants to explain where I am, naturally. I cannot stay here forever."

"When are you planning… to return to your father?"

"Soon." She twisted a cloth, did not meet his gaze. "I go next week, I think. I must now take a fast liner and take an airplane across the Continent so that I am not too late. It will not be easy to go where I want to go."

He stared at her, and his jaw hardened. "How about letting me go with you? I can see you through."

"Oh, never! It is much too dangerous, for you, for me, for my own people. You do not know the languages, the intrigues, the spies. Never would I think of it!"

He made a wry face. "We'll skip that then. But I'll be over later."

"No!" she said vehemently. "I will refuse to see you. I forbid you."

"You, Stephanie? Refuse to see me?"

And her face suddenly was contorted, and her mouth was trembling, and she was crying on his coat lapels. "Do you think I will wish to torture myself? It is hard enough here, how do you think it will be there? You do not believe me when I say that I must stay beside my father? You do not know the obedience, the love and respect and deference that women of my country give to a father. We have, in certain parts of my country, still the *harem* and the wearing of the veil. It is like that.

"It is impossible to explain to an American. But I think I should die if I ever, how do you call it, let him down, my father. There is where I am needed first, and there I must go. So I should refuse if you came to see me, for it would be too cruel."

He held her tightly, not saying anything. It was hard for an American to appreciate, truly, yet he felt the tremendous force of an old tradition working upon her, and he sensed the proud humility of her sacrifice. For all his will and desire it prevailed against him, and he knew it. He kissed her and walked out of the room, and his heart was bleak and gray and sullenly angry.

14

MYSTERIOUS TUNNEL

THROGG'S NECK WAS a long ride by subway and street car from downtown Manhattan. It was late afternoon when he finally arrived in the neighborhood of the monumental works. It adjoined a cemetery in a scantily settled corner of the East Bronx. The works consisted of a small shop and a spacious yard, in which finished gravestones were on display in front, and where blocks of stone in various stages of cutting, lay scattered all over. A big bare house rested further back, flanked by a well-cultivated kitchen garden, and a field.

Ward wore the collar of his light overcoat turned up, his hat brim low, and he was grateful for the dusk, so rapidly falling. He walked past the place, glanced at a few men in overalls cleaning up. Angelo was not among them. He continued, sizing up the neighborhood, and made for a small restaurant half a block from the Bellini place.

He was inside the restaurant and on a stool at the horse-shoe counter before he took special note of the young man exchanging raucous gibes with the chef. The young man, in a sweater and cap, with a cup of coffee in one hand, lounged on the counter opposite Ward with an air of old acquaintance. Ward took one look and ducked his head, absorbed in a menu on which he did not even see the words. The young man was Angelo Bellini.

It was a delicate, dangerous situation. Bellini, once he recognized Ward, would surely be frightened into desperate action. But Ward had infinitely less fear of the fellow than he had of miscarriage of his plans. He wished to remain unobserved, simply so that he might do all the observing himself. He reached inside his coat, casually loosened the gun in its holster, drew forth a fresh handkerchief, and flipping it open, held it to his face as if nursing an eye sore from a cinder. He subjected the unsuspecting gunman to a discreet, cold, one-eyed scrutiny.

Bellini was totally unaware and unsuspicious; He was among friends, friends who had an inkling of his real employment and a considerable awe of it.

WARD ORDERED A meal at random and, bending over his plate, ate slowly, studiously, lacking appetite. He stalled, prolonging the process, listening to the meaningless banter, grimly waiting. It was fully twenty minutes later before Bellini finished the coffee and felt an impulse to go.

The boss of the place, a lean, brisk, grinning Latin, said, "You go to the dance in Tremont tonight, Angelo?"

"Me? Oh, no! That bunch of palookas?"

"Some nice girls there. You don't come around often enough. You don't know what you miss, Angelo."

"Nuts!" said Angelo succinctly. "Playing music for six years, I don't miss much. I got to meet a guy tonight."

The boss grinned. "You make some money, eh?"

"Plenty, plenty. I know where it grows on trees."

"You show me sometime, huh?"

"Sure, sure."

*Ward worked him
over effectively*

"Well, you go downtown tonight, eh, Angelo? Come back soon. Glad to see you."

"I'll be around," said Angelo from the door. "I'm meeting this guy uptown. See you tomorrow."

Ward turned that morsel over in his mind. Meeting the guy uptown. Odd—and interesting. And it promised an active evening, rather than a cold, futile vigil while Angelo remained in the bosom of his family. Ward paid the check and went outside.

It would soon be dark. He strolled about the neighborhood, never leaving the Bellini home entirely out of sight. Presently, when the shadows were deep and gave shelter, he took a post among some shrubbery at the entrance to the cemetery. A street light glowed immediately in front of the Bellini property, and he had an excellent view of the house and all around it. He set himself patiently to wait.

Bellini came out of the house with the slamming of a screen door about an hour later. He lit a cigarette, thrust hands deep in coat pockets, and set out along the sidewalk,

breasting the stiff cool breeze sweeping in off Long Island
Sound. Ward was baffled at the direction he took. He was
heading east, pushing further into the barely settled vicinity that lay toward the Sound. Ward followed, at a loss for
explanation, but determined to find one as soon as possible.

IT WAS QUITE a walk. Luckily the increasing growth of
trees and brush alongside the sidewalks afforded Ward
shelter and deep shadow. Bellini strode on without suspicion. He cut across a field. He followed a dirt road; came
to a long brick wall along the road, the enclosure to the
grounds of what was fifty years ago a luxurious gentleman's
estate, and which now, decrepit and abandoned, waited
in lonely patience for a realty boom and subdivision into
building lots. The shore along here held many such relics.

Bellini opened the iron gate giving on the grounds.
Ward, after quick debate, set himself, leaped, and climbed
atop the brick wall. Through denuded trees, he made
out the gunman striding up the path to the out-moded,
gingerbread-style, enormous house. No light shone in any
window. Notwithstanding, Bellini knocked on the door,
waited, talked a little through the panels, and then slipped
inside as the door opened for him. There were sounds of
subdued, acrimonious argument, shut off as the door was
closed.

Ward did not stir for some moments. The hunch was
strong that he had stumbled on something big. Not stumbled, precisely, for this was a cool, deliberate plan. It was
maturing with unexpected speed. Ward was calmly, coldly
pleased.

Were this house innocent, there would be light visible within. Were Bellini an infrequent visitor, his manner

would scarcely have been so self-assured. Ward, with only one misgiving, the fear of roving dogs, dropped from the wall to earth. He moved cautiously, uneasily, among the trees, exploring the place.

The grounds, he found, were spacious. They were pretty unkempt, but traces of old cultivation were noticeable. Eastward of the great house was an ornament typical of that day, a sunken garden, thick now with a rank growth of underbrush and weeds. Northward a noble sweep of sloping lawn ran down to a beach on the Sound. There was a small dock. Beyond, the water shimmered with the reflection of distant lights on the Long Island shore.

No dogs turned up, so Ward made a swift, extensive survey. On the beach, he paused a while, studying the darkness out over the water. He detected something there, something tall that swayed and gently brushed the obscure stars. It was a mast. There were three masts. And suddenly his straining vision made out the vague lines of a schooner swinging at anchor.

A lean, swift schooner, such as might well be powered by a potent Diesel auxiliary engine.

Ward went back to the house, the blood coursing faster in his veins with the vehement ardor of discovery. He approached close to the house, to examine the windows, to listen acutely for a telltale sound, to exercise that sheerest animal instinct, an unreasoning awareness of the hidden presence of men. The windows were all blank, empty, encrusted by the dust and rain of years. There was no clue, no sign. But there were men and lights and danger somewhere within these walls, all too cunningly concealed. The place smelled of the sinister, of death and devastation.

A rustling, and the crackling of brittle twigs, brought Ward to a frigid halt. He pressed close to the house, his gaze darting hotly through the darkness. The sound came from the sunken garden. Two men climbed the steps to the lawn, conversing in hoarsely subdued tones. They passed very close to Ward, unsuspicious and unaware.

"That damned tunnel!" one said angrily. "What's the matter with the front door?"

"What's the matter with you?" snarled the other. "The tunnel don't cost you no money, does it?"

"Aw, nuts! This creeping around is crazy. Who's gonna see, up here?"

"I suppose you want a butler opening the door for you? Well, shut up, or you'll have a screw at the Big Stony opening a cell door for you every morning in the year! You and the palooka. If you don't get your skulls cracked before that."

"Who's gonna do the cracking?" The cautious one laughed hollowly, sneering his contempt. They passed out of hearing, still arguing.

AND NOW WARD understood the reason for the acrimony at the door as Bellini was admitted. There was a tunnel somewhere, to be used in preference to the door. And there were those of the gang who nursed a swollen sense of their own importance and invincibility, and recklessly availed themselves of the door. Ward was grimly appreciative. Had Bellini vanished in the sunken garden, he doubted that he could have solved the mystery in the confusing darkness.

Ward went to the garden. Slowly, guardedly, he descended the steps, and moved about, pausing, pressing further, studying as best he might, the lay-out of the depressed area. The ground, he found, was entirely solid earth. There was a sun-dial in the center of the garden, and a long-dry fountain in the concrete wall at one end, a marble bowl set in a massive bronze panel in the wall, with a small nude figure in bas-relief holding a tilted vase, from which water once had streamed. Ward could just make out the design.

After a moment, Ward took hold of the bronze vase. It was instinctive; his mind groped for clues. He heaved on it, testing the solidity of the whole fountain. The vase moved under the pull of his hand.

He made greater exertion—and the entire metal panel moved, eerily, swinging without a sound on well-oiled hinges. It was a door, skillfully balanced, and built solidly into the wall. Beyond the door loomed an opening, and darkness.

Ward stepped warily into the darkness. He listened. There was only silence. He took out his pocket flash-light. The beam revealed a bare, concrete tunnel, dry and solid-looking. A few yards ahead, the tunnel turned at a right angle. Ward walked to the turn, A few feet again, and the tunnel resumed its original direction, straight for the house. There seemed to be no reason for this staggered construction. But there was a reason, and Ward guessed it in an instant.

Whoever had first built this secret passage, built it so that direct gunfire would not command it. Scrutinizing the concrete more closely, Ward estimated that it was laid down some time before the beginning of the century, perhaps even so far back as the Civil War. New York had been a hotbed of Copperhead intrigue in that day.

The second length of tunnel came to an end at a massive iron door. Ward eyed it from the tunnel angle, but went no further. There was hard satisfaction in him. This was no schooner, to vanish as soon as discovered. He went out of the tunnel, pushing the bronze door shut. It came to rest with a tiny click. The click disturbed him; he pulled again on the door. It swung open readily. He concluded that the thing was as finely balanced as a jeweled watch, but left unlocked.

Ward made his way out of the garden. He returned to the house, and circled it again, this time in search of cellar windows which might be revealing. He found no difference between them and the upper windows, and left off. Enough for one night, one man.

He took a last look at the sinister old house from the iron gate, and then set out back the way he had come, walking swiftly. There would be other nights.

WHEN WARD RETURNED to South Street, he found the hide-out dark and deserted. A note from Stephanie pinned to his pillow, explained that she had gone home to Brooklyn, and gave him farewell and good luck. It did not specify whether the farewell was final or merely for the moment. There was no sign or word of Teverson. Ward, not yet entirely up to the mark, was tired out after his Bronx adventure, too weary to care tonight. He turned in, and slept.

Events began to stir next day. The morning shipping list reported the expected arrival of the S.S. *Caliban,* out of Barcelona, about noon. And when Ward telephoned Hymie Holtz, to announce the satisfactory conclusion of the Throgg's Neck job, Holtz was serious and mystifying.

"Ward, you are to me like one of the boys here. They give me the break, I give them the break. There is something very important. I want you should come up here positively right away."

"What is it? Job? Couldn't take it, Hymie."

"It's nothing so small potatoes as a job," said Hymie, with a note of grimness. "Don't you do nothing first. Come here to my office in a hurry."

Ward, deeply puzzled and touched by foreboding, reviewed the possibilities, but could hazard no guess as to Holtz's "something." He looked in on Teverson, saw him in deep sleep, and left him undisturbed. He went out, stopped for a cup of coffee at a lunch counter, and took the subway uptown.

The sternness of Hymie Holtz's face attested to the seriousness of his news. He looked at Ward across the desk, fingering a little sheaf of papers.

"You tell me honestly, Ward. Are you now in a racket?"

Ward shrugged. "You might call it that."

"Are you hiding? Do the police know where you are?"

Ward looked at him steadily, coldly. "Don't ask so many questions, Hymie. What's on your mind? If I want to answer questions afterward, I'll let you bow."

Holtz grunted, shuffling the papers. "It is my business to deal in strict confidence with my clients, Ward. But sometimes there comes a case where I am not certain which way confidence and friendship goes. This is one. I am retained in professional capacity by clients who want I should find some guys. So I do a job, and I find them. The names were not known, but I learn them. And the name of one of them is—Dexter Ward!"

Ward lit a cigarette, blew a cloud of smoke at the ceiling. Hymie could read nothing in that cold, expressionless face. Ward said, "I'm listening."

"My clients are two men," said Hymie. "Foreigners they are. They have only the license plate number of a taxicab. They tell me a kind of crazy story about chasing that cab one night, with shooting, with full speed through the East Side, and a cop firing at them. They do not want to be killed for bandits, they say, so they beat it. But they recognized a notorious criminal of the Old Country in that taxicab, and they want to make an arrest for extradition. They tell me to find the cab, locate the driver, dig from him a story, trace the passengers, learn where they live—and they will do the rest."

"So?"

"So I don't have much trouble. The cab is easy, the time-book at the garage shows the driver, and he is like butter when the heat is turned on him a little. He sends us to the cab starter at the Hotel Blassingame, with details and descriptions, and after a while the starter puts it all together for us. I am hot now, very close—but I am all of a sudden very cold personally, when a bellhop tells me in strict confidence that the fellow in the cab with the pretty girl that night is not the name the hotel tells me at all, but is really a guy by the name of Dex Ward, which he has heard often.

"I find the story my clients tell me is all wet, I find a murder. I find Dex Ward and somebody named Teverson has disappeared. I find I am getting practically into Police Department territory. So I call off all bets until I know where I am going. Maybe now you feel more like answering some questions, eh?"

WARD WAS SILENT a moment, thinking, then he said, "A girl called you while I was laid up, Hymie, didn't she?"

"Yes, and even if I was worried a little at first, she honeyed me out of it. She knew all our business."

"She's a smart girl. I think you'd like her."

"I can tell she's a smart girl, and I like her voice. But what should it matter to you if I like her or not?"

Ward said dryly, "She's the girl who was in the cab with me. Your two clients spotted her, and did their damnedest to assassinate her. Her father was the former prime minister of Berengaria, and now a fugitive. Your clients are secret police of the present dictator, assigned to kill her. How do you like those mess of tomatoes, Mr. Holtz?"

Holtz's eyes narrowed, and he studied Ward. Then he swore, a rare event. "The dirty crooks I Foreigners, they are—I should help them murder somebody! I'll hand them back the retainer and tell them it's no onions, I can't find nothing."

"Tell them that story, and they'll hire some other agency to go to work. Then she and I will both be in the pickle jar. Keep the retainer, and hand them a stiff bill—and deliver a report about a couple of other guys."

Hymie thought, nodded vigorously. "You're right. A couple of other guys. They just sailed for China, if I ain't mistaken."

"That's swell, Hymie!" Ward smiled for the first time. "Now, suppose you tell me where they're located in town?"

"They live at—" and Hymie stopped. *Why?*

"I've never lied to you, Hymie, have I?" Ward said. "If that girl is missing, I want to know where to look."

"Well…" Hymie scratched his head. The reason looked

very valid. "All right, I'll tell you. If there's a shooting, or bad trouble, and they hang any part of it on me, don't forget I'll hound you, Ward! These two men have a cheap apartment in a tenement off First Avenue in Yorkville. It looked funny to me that two men with plenty of money should live there, but I see now why they keep away from hotels, where they would be noticed. I give you the names and address." He scribbled a memorandum and handed it to Ward.

"You're a pal, Hymie," said Ward, glancing at the names. They were—Kondar and Stuban, with unpronounceable names.

Hymie cleared his throat, and said, "That murder, now? That Arabian fellow? You answering any questions about that?"

"Only one. If you ask me did I kill the poor devil, I'll say no."

"**SUCH A PAL!** Such a gratitude!" Hymie sighed. "Well, some day I ask again, maybe you feel like talking. And that reminds me, I had a long talk with a funny old guy while you were laid up. He comes here because you mentioned my name. He tells me all his life he has been fascinated by a detective, and he hopes I don't mind the intrusion, and we talk shop for more than one hour, and I find he is one amazing guy. I could even give him a job!"

Ward stared, frowning. "Doctor Beecher! What did he want?"

"To meet a detective, I'm telling you. He talked about you a little. I couldn't get him to talk more. But he thinks you are one swell guy. He would like to be in your shoes, at your age. He thinks he should have been a detective."

Hymie paused, and said impressively, "And you know what?"

Ward began to grin. "What?"

"I am invited up to his place to drop in for tea!" impressively. "Tea—I gave you my word."

Ward laughed. The picture was too good—Hymie and the gentle doctor, engaged in bloodthirsty discourse, sedately drinking tea!

15

EMERGENCY CALL

WARD RETURNED DIRECTLY to South Street. He found Teverson in brooding mood, cross-legged on the floor of the big room, surrounded by outspread newspapers and a litter of guns and gun parts. One of the weapons was that lethal masterpiece, the Thompson subcaliber machine gun. Teverson had a pan of cleaning fluid and a can of fine oil, and he was conditioning the guns. He also had a tumbler half full of whisky.

"Planning a massacre, Tev?"

"I'm cutting out paper dolls, sweetheart," Tev said sarcastically.

"How about the stuff on the *Caliban?*"

"That's up your alley. It's none of my affair."

"Why not? It used to be."

Teverson looked at him with eyes that were a little bloodshot. He snarled, "What's on your mind? You backing out?"

"Hell, no!" calmly. "Just curious."

"You've no reason to be. I've explained at length. This is penny ante. And certain death for pay-off. When I played, I played the field on the nose and no limit. When I quit, I quit."

"For good?"

"Dex, if I could tell which way the dice were going to fall on the next roll I wouldn't be sitting here, so stop asking questions."

The man was intrenched behind a wall, and he would admit no one. Ward gave up.

Ward soon went out again. He walked across to the old ferry house, ancient and unrepaired in its retirement, closed off from the street by a tall picket fence. Here and there individual pickets were missing. On impulse, Ward slipped through one of the gaps, and walked out to the vacant ferry slip. He saw a cat-walk atop the embanked pilings that formed the sides of the slip, and climbing a ladder to the cat-walk, walked out to the farthest point of the tottering structure, overlooking a vast expanse of the East River.

It was a clear, fair day, one of those rare autumn days when the air is fresher than city air has any right to be, and the sun brighter, and the soaring towers and the bright colors and the very immensity of the city are things of joy.

Ward felt the sun's warmth, smelled the fair, good smell of the harbor at full tide, sweeping fresh from the sea, was beguiled by that mystic inspiration of the day. He ceased to ask questions of himself, to plague his soul with doubts. Life was a pattern too haphazard and involved to reduce to comprehensible terms, a pattern simply to be lived as the fates designed it.

But there was no negation in it, no dry rot or decay. It was ultimately good, regardless of inscrutable design. That a man had enemies was good, for they guaranteed that his life would be a full one. Pain and struggle were the price of living. That it rained was good, and that a man hungered, and it was even good that there was death in the world.

Then suddenly Ward thought of Stephanie, in rain and perhaps in hunger, in struggle and perhaps defeat, at a bivouac with Death in some lonely mountain pass five thousand miles away. And in an instant the day was rent, and the peace was gone, and there was only a blind, restive, unspent fury of resentment. He turned away from the murmuring sun-bright river and walked quickly back along the catwalk, and made his way to the street.

Ward hailed a cab and rode to Bowling Green. There he entered the imposing old Custom House, to run a gantlet of minor functionaries to a small private office occupied by an athletic, competent looking man of Ward's own age, who jumped up from his desk in surprise and pleasure, and made Ward warmly welcome.

They talked of other days, of four-years-no-see-you, of sports and business and old friends who had made conquests of wealth or fame.

"The reasons why I haven't been around sooner, Dan," said Ward, "are numerous. Also perfectly good, every one. I've been in some strange places and done some peculiar things, and some day I'll tell you all about it. Right now I'm in need of some confidential information, and I think you can give it to me."

"Mighty glad to, if the assumption is correct. What is it? Income tax?"

"It's not in your department But perhaps you can get it through inside channels without starting a row, I happen to know a pair of citizens of Berengaria who are in town. I don't know them well enough to find out directly if they are here on alien permits or if by legal entry. Can you have them looked up?"

"Can do. Day or so."

WARD TOOK PENCIL and paper and copied from Hymie's memorandum the names of the two Berengarian agents, Kondar and Stuban. He did not add the address. "I merely want to know their standing in the U.S., Dan. I'm not cracking down on anybody, so I won't include their whereabouts or other details."

"Not necessary. If these are the names, and they're listed, we'll have all the information required. If they're not… well, do as you please about that."

"Good lad! I'll drop in or call you for a report."

Ward went next to a drug store telephone booth, and called the Brooklyn pier at which the *Caliban* was due. The ship was an hour in port, already unloading. He looked up the number of Callahan's tavern, and called there, inquiring if any of the men from the *Caliban* were in the place. He was asked who wanted to know, and at mention of the magic name Teverson, was told there were five of them restively waiting.

Ward took the subway to Brooklyn, in order to pick a Brooklyn-bred cab driver when he emerged. The driver knew Callahan's, and had him there in five minutes. It was an old fashioned saloon in the middle of a dingy block underneath a grimy old Elevated structure, a place that had mysteriously survived the rigors of prohibition intact, even to the fly-specked mirrors.

"I phoned here just a few minutes ago," Ward told the tall, powerful looking man; behind the bar. "Where will I find the *Caliban* crowd?"

Blue eyes fixed him keenly. "And who might you be, mister?"

"A friend of Teverson's. I'm handling this myself."

The man wiped the bar for a moment in enigmatic silence. "Tev ought to be here. Too damn many funny things happening these days. Well… go through that door into the back room and you'll find them."

The five were killing time in the room at the rear, three at cards and two with newspapers. They all gazed at Ward with something closer to hostility than welcome. They were all in shore clothes, clean and fit looking men, a little hard around the mouth and about weathered eyes. The biggest of the lot, a long-armed, blond Scandinavian, seemed to be their spokesman. He was in a contentious mood.

"We've always done our business direct with Teverson," he said flatly, after Ward introduced himself. "Why not this time?"

Ward explained. Teverson was too well known to certain enemies, it was too dangerous. He said coolly, "You might say he's taken in a partner. This particular transaction was in my hands from the start."

The big fellow grunted, unmoved.

"Did you have any trouble coming ashore?" Ward asked.

"We came five together to make sure we didn't. I've heard talk of trouble. And you can be damned well certain, mister, I'm going to steer clear of it!"

"Excellent idea!" Ward drawled. Anger was stirring in him; the big man's truculence was more than mere suspicion warranted. "Now suppose we get down to business."

Ward placed before him on the table the inventory-memorandum. One of the others picked up several small packages from the floor and laid them on the table. A second man leaned over to study the memorandum. The big man sat gazing at Ward like a thunder cloud. And abruptly he exploded; he swept the packages back to the floor and struck the table a blow.

"No! We'll do no business here! I want to see Teverson and nobody else. I'll deal with no damned four-flushing, chiseling lubber on earth."

"Meaning," Ward said politely, "me?"

"I do!"

COMPOSEDLY WARD FOLDED the inventory and replaced it in his pocket. He buttoned his coat. He got up. "Well, I guess that's that. It suits me. But before we part I must insist on one purely personal satisfaction."

He walked casually around the table; followed by puzzled eyes. Abruptly he grabbed the coat lapels of the big fellow, hauled him violently upright, and struck him a short, clipped, pile-driving blow squarely on the heavy chin. It was quicker than thought, efficient and effective. The huge frame sagged; Ward dragged the unconscious man to the wall and lowered him to a seated position on the floor.

"He talks too much!" said Ward in a tone quiet and hard, challenging consequences. "When he comes to, tell him I said so."

And then he noticed that the other four, astonished and motionless, were all suddenly grinning, as if in spite of themselves. Their eyes were wide with wonder and delight. One broke into outright laughter, and the others joined him. It was seagoing laughter, hale and heartfelt. Ward was nonplused.

A red-headed small man with an amiably ugly face said, "Faith, and he does, too! He admires to hear himself, that man. Mister, I never saw a sweeter blow struck!"

One of the others, still chuckling, and gazing at Ward with approval, said, "He had it coming. He just tried the high hand once too often. I vote we leave him there and talk this thing over. I'm not here for my health; I want some money."

That practical reminder of their purpose carried appeal for all of them. That calm, unpremeditated and wholly justifiable knockout was a passport to their confidence. The air was cleared, and Ward sat down with them and offered fuller explanation, and they listened. When a man was doing the talking they gave ready ears.

Ten minutes later, with an understanding established, Ward was counting out small piles of money from his bank roll. The big fellow was back again at the table, silent, sullen, routed, still trying to figure out what had happened to him. He rubbed his jaw and watched Ward covertly with a puzzled, baffled expression. The door opened, and the tall bartender sailed briskly into the room bearing a tray with six beers.

"On the house," he growled, low-voiced. "I needed an alibi to come in here. In the last ten minutes, six mean looking mugs have drifted into the place, one by one, and they're all standing around staring into their beer without sounding off a word. Make what you want of it, but I don't like their looks."

"Any signs of guns on them?" Ward asked.

"They ain't showing any, but I got my own opinion."

"Hm. Is there a back way out of here?"

"Not without passing through the barroom, friend. I think you got a hot one on your hands. Try and get out without no shooting in my place!"

And grimly, discreetly, he hastened back to his bar.

WARD GRIPPED THE edge of the table, swearing inwardly, silently. The thing was sharply clear. The incoming ship had been watched, of course. Five men in a bunch were too many to tackle, but they had been trailed, and a call for reïnforcements immediately telephoned. Besides the six in the saloon, there were probably additional reserves planted outside on the street and in the rear of the place.

"Boys," Ward snapped, "they're not going to take this away from me!"

"Easy does it, mister!" the red-head cautioned. "We have no guns among us. If you have, that's still six to one." They all watched him, touched with uneasy doubt, counting on him. Ward got up. He went decisively to the telephone in a corner, put a nickel in the slot, dialed the operator.

"I want to report a fire," he snapped. A brief pause, and he rattled off a report of a veritable holocaust consuming Mike Callahan's old saloon, with occupants of the building entrapped by the flames and in dire peril. The report was accepted without question, and there was a tight, hard smile on Ward's mouth as he replaced the receiver. There'd be action in a matter of minutes.

"What the hell—?" said the redhead.

"I hate to disappoint a fireman," said Ward, "but somebody's got to help us out of here."

He began to stow the smaller packages in convenient pockets.

The response to the fire alarm was miraculously swift.

They sat around the table, ears straining for the sound of the thundering apparatus, and they soon caught the shrill whistle of the first engine arriving. Inside three seconds more, the street outside was filled with the urgent clamor of giant motors and unlimbering gear.

Ward opened the door slightly. Into the saloon charged a squad of helmeted men, the skirmishers, armed with axes and crowbars. A lieutenant, suspicious and already angry, demanded, "Where's this damned fire?"

"Fire?" repeated the bewildered bartender. "What fire?"

Ward grinned, baring a thin line of hard white teeth, and nodded to the five men at the table. He picked up the remainder of the packages, and led the way out of the room. The lieutenant was declaring his wrathy opinion of the person who had reported the nonexistent blaze. The place was full of firemen, and no one paid much attention to Ward. The half dozen hard-faced customers in the tavern looked embarrassed and sullen, but they studiously refrained from looking at Ward and his five companions.

Ward edged his way through the cluster of firemen in the door. Outside he paused to engage one in talk. After a few casual questions, he said in an earnest, confidential tone, "Don't drag me into this, chief, but let me give you a tip. A couple of those muggs at the bar are behind this. There was a bet made as to how many minutes it would take you to get here."

The fireman looked at him sharply. "Which of them?"

Ward shook his head firmly. "I'm not getting mixed up in it. I'm just giving you a steer. Make the most of it."

The fireman stared hard, then pushed his determined way into the saloon. Ward, with his wary, formidable looking five grouped compactly around him, walked down the street. A policeman, ardently forming fire lines around the zone of presumable danger, roared at them and sped them on their way. They obediently hastened.

16

WATERFRONT WAR

HALF AN HOUR later Ward descended from a taxicab at the bronze gates of Dr. Beecher's museum. Ward was admitted this time without delay, and alone with Beecher he unloaded the packages, arraying them on the desk.

The good doctor gazed at them with avid eyes.

"A new shipment, Ward?"

"So new I haven't even opened them, Doc."

"Are they for me?"

"Some may be."

"What are they? Let me open them."

Ward shoved the more bulky packages across to the doctor, and smiled as he watched the man tear at the wrappings in a fever of impatience.

Ward spent an hour with Dr. Beecher. "These items are a little too diversified in character for us to keep here," he told Ward. "Besides, I'm of the opinion that you will get a better cash total by offering them singly to the proper agencies."

He offered suggestions. The small jewel casket, a Cellini: piece probably, he'd like to bid in on himself. The exquisite miniature monstrance of diamond-studded gold should arouse the covetousness of a certain collector in Toledo.

The famous Hay collection in St. Louis would be decidedly interested in the Medici silver toilet set, a quaint, intricately molded group of accessories to beauty, mirror, combs and other items, once plied by some Renaissance lady of quality.

"I'm sorry for the people who had to part with these things," he said gently, fondling the lovely little monstrance.

"These dizzy years seem to be benefiting some of us," drawled Ward. "I am willing to help both sides. You'll do all sides a great service if you'll put these things in your safe until I'm better prepared to handle them."

"With pleasure, my boy. I'll gladly be of service in any way I can."

Ward entrusted the entire shipment to Beecher's care, including the packets of bank notes in Spanish, French and English currency.

It was dusk when Ward let himself into the house on South Street. He entered quietly, and stood for a moment in the dark kitchen, listening.

Teverson was furiously busy within, running, slamming doors, his activity suggestive of emergency. Ward went through to the front.

On a settee two traveling bags lay open. One was full of clothes and personal effects, jammed in without regard for order. The other contained packages of money and a collection of arms and ammunition, Teverson appeared from his room, carrying more clothes. There was a kind of grim ferocity in him.

"What's this?" Ward inquired. "Moving day?"

Teverson grunted. "I'm getting out of here."

"Where to?"

"Greece, most likely."

"May I ask why?"

Teverson did not reply. He disappeared again into his room. Ward poured a small drink, sat down and crossed his long legs. There was a faint smile on his face and a frosty glint in his eyes.

When Teverson reappeared he thrust at Ward a large envelope.

"Drafts," he said. "On the money remaining to my accounts in five separate depositories. You'll have need of it. Call it a loan; and I'll draw on you later."

"Greece!" said Ward reflectively. "We have no very effective extradition treaty with Greece, have we?"

"We haven't."

"Would you mind telling me what's happened?"

TEVERSON PAUSED IN his headlong activity. He snarled, "I've been framed: Thoroughly jobbed and sold! The Federals caught a whole case of Bulgarian narcotics coming in, consigned to me. They made arrests, and the prisoners have all confessed that they were acting under my orders, and that wholesale shipments of cocaine and heroin have been landed through me for the past two years."

"Through you! They're taking a rap voluntarily—on a false confession?"

"Under orders from The Eel, unquestionably, and in fear of their lives."

"Where did you pick up this news?"

"At the Dockloaders'. A longshoremen's hangout on West Street, I went looking for news and got more than I bargained for. The Federal men raided a tramp freighter from the Near East about dawn this morning, and seized the stuff. The story is all over the waterfront. They knew the junk's been coming in wholesale, but couldn't locate the leak. The Eel located it for them, deliberately. It's a sweet case, with evidence and confessions and the damning fact that I'm already classed a fugitive. So I'm clearing out. Bucking the Federal Government along with everyone else is not my idea of any way to make a living."

"And what would you suggest that I do?"

"Anything you please. I'm clearing out."

Ward sighed, shifted a little in the chair. "Well, I regret the necessity, but you force me to tell you that you're not clearing out."

Teverson whirled. "Who's to stop me?"

"I am," Ward snapped. Deliberately he spun and leveled the deadly little .25.

Teverson glared at the automatic, at Ward, speechless.

Ward said, "Sit down. You did me a similar favor once. I'll return it."

"You owe me no favors!"

"Sit down!" Ward repeated ominously.

Teverson hesitated, but he sat down. He looked feline, like a cat waiting to spring.

Ward said in clipped, hard speech, "You've been regretting our bargain for some days, Tev. You won't talk reasonably, and you've been riding me pretty roughly. Instead of getting over it, you're taking the sudden run-out powder. Before you leave here, you're going to do some explaining."

Teverson said nothing, staring steadily.

Ward smiled, with a shading of contempt. "You've changed, Tev. I thought I knew you, but I was mistaken. You can't take it. You act hard, Tev, and you preach a gospel of hardness, but you're not hard." He paused. "You're yellow!"

Teverson's face slowly drained of color and he breathed deeply, but his opaque gaze was unflinching.

Ward went on, "When you took me in, broke and down to bedrock, you were tops in your racket. You hazed me with little mercy. You said, if I recall, that I was never man enough to go take what I wanted from the world."

Teverson snarled, "You *weren't* man enough! You let the world throw you, and you stayed thrown. I knew what you needed. I hazed you—deliberately. I let you in for a taste of real trouble. It was rough treatment, and necessary."

"Quite likely. But if you diagnosed my case so well, how is it you fail so badly with your own?"

TEVERSON CAME WILDLY to his feet. Now he looked fit to spring, but deterred, perhaps, by the gun. He paced the floor, goaded mercilessly by the mysterious canker in his soul.

"Fail! Yellow! Look here. How much do you think you know about me? In the years we ran together, I came to know you like a book, but you never figured me out. I couldn't let you. I didn't dare. Well, here's the truth now. I told you I had no family. Did I ever tell you that I ran away from an orphanage at fifteen? That I chiseled and cheated and plotted and pushed my way up in the world from absolute scratch?

"It took brains and a conscience of cast iron, but I did it. Did it ever occur to you that the money that carried me along with a millionaire's son throughout all Europe was money I made by my wits? That I even framed that fool in Paris with marked cards?"

Ward stared, and there was concentration of thought in his eyes, but no other expression.

Teverson went on, "I've never taken a dime from a man who had real need of his dime. I took over fools and those with too many dimes, I never took you for a cent, though you tempted me."

"Thanks," dryly.

"Through all those years you never once suspected the envy that was a corrosive inside me. I took care you didn't. It wasn't personal. It was envy of your easy wealth, your station, in life, your bright future. I wanted those things. How was I to get them? By slaving for forty years? Not I! You hadn't, and I wouldn't. I wanted them right then—*right now!* And I got them! I got them the hard way. And you say I'm yellow?"

"You can skip that, Tev," Ward said. "It started you talking, which was my intention. You have the talent for getting what you want, to an extraordinary degree. Granted. But getting what you want is one thing—*keeping* what you've got is another. That might be said to be equally true of money, or music—or friendship."

Teverson was silent. He did not look at Ward.

Ward went on. "I lost a fortune myself. But it wasn't mine. I hadn't worked or fought for a dollar of it I've had to learn a great deal indeed about getting things these few years, and I'm still bitterly learning. But I'll have to be six feet under, now or any time, with a ton of marble holding me down, before I'll willingly let anyone take from me what I've fought for and earned with this head and these two hands!"

Teverson was slow to answer, and the tone was quiet.

"Well; you've got something now. How are you going to go about keeping it?"

"By doing no more than you'd do, if you'd go to work on it!" Ward declared passionately. "You're quitting, and you won't even try to fight. I've never seen you actually crawl before, and I can't take it without an argument—even if I had to back it with a gun. What in hell's got into you?"

Teverson looked at him. He sat thinking. There was a cooler light in the bitter dark eyes, a took of sanity and clear, unimpeded vision, disillusioned, even faintly wistful. It was a remarkable expression for Teverson.

"Dex, there's something to explain that you might have guessed, since you are analyzing me so thoroughly. It can be told in a few words...."

Suddenly a peculiar tension flickered across the man's face. He looked up toward the ceiling, his very nostrils aquiver as all his senses instantly attuned themselves to danger.

"Listen!"

WARD FELT THE contagion of alarm. From above, from the roof, came a sound. Many sounds, tiny, almost inaudible, sinister.

Teverson stood up. For an instant he stood poised, listening. Then he reached swiftly into the open traveling bag, snatched up the Thompson gun and a drum of cartridges. He clicked the drum into place, waited, watching the skylight. He cursed softly.

"Come on, you creeping vermin!"

"Easy, Tev! May be nothing."

"Nothing, hell! Close that bag with the money and guns. Take it out by the escape shaft."

Ward snapped the bag shut, ran into the kitchen with it. He opened the shaft door, wedged the bag in the opening.

Abruptly the quiet ended with a sharp shattering of glass. It came from the skylight. There was a heavy thud on the floor. Almost instantly followed the stunning rip and thunder of the machine gun. Ward looked, saw Teverson with the gun throbbing, roaring, spraying the skylight with a hail of lead.

Then Ward saw something else. A small, cylindrical object lying on the rug in the center of the room. A tiny plume of smoke escaped from it.

"*Gas!*" He leaped for the front room, for Teverson. "Gas, Tev! Get out of here. *Get out!*"

He seized the murderously intent man, snapped the safety on the gun, silencing it. He pulled the gun from Teverson's hands, hurled him toward the kitchen. Then he snatched up the telephone, switched off the lights in the room, and retreated to the kitchen, slamming the door on the telephone cord as tightly as possible.

Beyond the door an instant after, there was an explosion, a hollow, liquid sound. Teverson began to curse lividly.

Twirling the telephone dial, Ward said, "Down the shaft, Tev! They'll have the house surrounded. You didn't lose that gang; they trailed you here."

"Come on! Come on!"

Ward listened to the deliberate drone on the telephone line. Already, filtering thinly into the room, poisoning the atmosphere, a sharp, stinging, lethal odor assailed them.

"Stephanie? Dex Ward. Get this—and move fast. Get your boat over here. They found the hide-out, and they're here in force. We're going down the shaft and out the

sewer. We'll wait in the old ferry slip and flash a light....
That's right. Get here before they figure it out and come
after us. Pound the bottom out of that boat!"

Slamming the receiver in place, he barked, "Go on,
Slide!"

Teverson took a firm grip on the bag, grabbed the
smooth pole in the shaft, and slid, vanishing instantly.

Ward, the Thompson gun in one hand, clung to the
pole long enough to make certain the stout steel door was
securely locked. Then he loosened his hold and dropped
like a plummet into cavernous darkness.

The interval of waiting in the ghostly old ferry house was
an endless suspense. When the gang penetrated into the
house, as they were unquestionably prepared to do, gas or
no gas, it would be only a matter of time before they solved
the mystery of their quarry's disappearance, and followed.
THEN FINALLY THEY heard the deep baying of the powerful motor over the waters. In another moment, the little
craft appeared, speeding straight for them. Stephanie's
man performed a daring maneuver, cutting the throttle,
spinning the wheel, and bringing the boat on a slithering
skid into the narrow slip in a welter of spray and white
water. He edged her close to the "apron" against which the
ferries had once come to rest. Ward and Teverson handed
down their burdens, and jumped into the cockpit. They
were instantly off again.

There was no talk. They were grim. They fled full speed.
The wind and the deep-toned exhaust filled their hearing.
Stephanie, tense with mingled fear and relief, sat close to
Dex Ward, hanging tightly on his arm, and he clung to the
seat as they bounced roughly over choppy cross tides. The

stars were remote and dim, and the darkness hung heavy over the glimmering waters.

It was a deeply stirred conclave that held council of war in Stephanie's place in that ensuing hour. Teverson, pacing up and down in insupportable inner turmoil, was a brand burning for vengeance, his apathy consumed in the flames. Ward, studying him shrewdly, was full of a hard private satisfaction. The enigma was not fully solved, but its outlines were clearer. A process stormy and soul-shaking was under way within Teverson, and the outcome might be momentous in all three of their lives.

"This has gone too far!" said Teverson. "I can't take it. I can't! I thought I could merely run out. But I can't take this."

Earnestly Stephanie said, "I think while you are on this earth, Tev, that man Eel will never be satisfied. He is a man with a great obsession. I think if you go to the ends of the world, some day will come a man with a gun, seeking you."

He grunted acknowledgment of that likelihood.

"What you do then?" she asked.

"Do?" Teverson looked at her grimly, glanced at Ward. There was a hint of hesitation and deference in his look. "You've been the idea man lately, Dex. What have you got to say?"

"Plenty!"

And he had, indeed, plenty. He told them the story of Dr. Beecher and Angelo Bellini, of Hymie Holtz and his skilled assistance, of the sinister old house behind the brick wall up on Throgg's Neck. He talked with vehemence: he had made strides, and was in no mood for half measures.

"To tackle this gang we need organization. Not merely a

gun mob. There must be a large number of men who have either profited by Teverson's activities or been hurt by those of The Eel. The dock and shipping men, waterfront folk. We should be able to cover the waterfront with a cordon of informers. They won't talk to the police out of fear, but they will to us. They trust Tev."

"And what will they have to tell us?" Teverson demanded.

"Primarily—the movements of the schooner. It must have attracted somebody's curiosity somewhere, and be a little bit known." Ward looked at his hands, powerful and impressive, flexing and clenching them. "I once told you, Tev, I'd guarantee to make those punks talk if I once got my grip on a couple. That schooner can be located. I tell you we can break down their racket. We'll use their own methods. I'll waylay The Eel's whole mob, man by man, if you'll back my play."

Teverson frowned. "You've already located the schooner, I mean at Throgg's Neck."

"That's not the place to tackle it. It's too dangerous. And furthermore, it's innocently at anchor. I want to see it downtown, away from its base and up to the ears in some kind of dirty work."

Resolution was marching, gathering in Teverson, yet he said, "It's a pretty one-sided business. And I'm not fond of the short end."

Stephanie reminded him, "You're not fond of dying, either, I think."

"No," said Teverson, "I'm not. And that's the final argument. We'll go to work on it!"

And Dex Ward smiled enigmatically, a bit dangerously.

But then he looked at Stephanie, and saw the dread and unhappiness all too incompletely hidden in her eyes, and the smile died a little, and his own eyes narrowed, and in the pupils there was a cold enduring hardness.

17

REVOLT

THEY CROSSED TO Manhattan early next day. The day was drear, a murk of mist and drizzle. Their immediate plans were simple, clear. First, to avoid trouble at all cost. Next, to clear the decks, to dispose of preliminaries. Teverson was to make cautious contact with his waterfront acquaintance and explain the situation, Ward was to clear up pending business detail. Both were to telephone Stephanie's place at set intervals, reporting progress and giving reassurance. They would meet there later.

Ward saw Teverson go off alone, not without misgiving. It was a dangerous mission. But the risk must be run.

Ward himself, for first step, had the fairly safe duty of running up to call on Dr. Beecher. He first got Señor Rondalvo on the telephone, made a rendezvous with him for later, and proceeded to Beecher's museum.

The doctor was delighted, and promptly produced the packets of currency Ward requested. He announced that he had sent off certain letters regarding the treasures still in his safe, and it was agreed to leave them there for the present.

"Teverson often allowed me to dispose of such things," he told Ward. "It is a very willing service."

"You'll be a shining light in the underworld soon, Doc," drawled Ward.

Beecher smiled. "I made an interesting acquaintance recently, Ward. I took the liberty of calling on a friend of yours."

"Hymie? So he told me."

They discussed Hymie, and then the doctor said with a certain hesitancy, "You understand my interest in such matters, so you'll pardon my curiosity, I hope. I'd like to ask a question. How did you get these things off the ship yesterday? And was there any trouble?"

Ward debated, wondering, but could see no harm in it. He told of the encounter at Callahan's. It made a good Story. Beecher would have pressed him for more, but Ward felt he was edging on dangerous ground. He stowed the packets in his pocket, pleaded pressing business, and took his leave.

Outside, Ward dropped into a drug store and called Brooklyn. Stephanie answered, and reported satisfactory word from Teverson. Ward took a cab downtown.

Rondalvo was waiting for him in a hotel lobby, and he escorted the *señor* to a modest little real estate office not far from Times Square.

"I've never been here," he told Rondalvo, "but Teverson made the arrangements for us. I gather it's headquarters for a big gambling syndicate."

"Gambling?" repeated the puzzled Rondalvo.

"The syndicate has a few side lines. They handle some gold held in private hands. They're private brokers in foreign exchange. They'll do anything with your money but print it for you. I'll get you some good American cash, or arrange for foreign drafts, just as your people wish."

"I commence to see now," said the other. "My Barcelona friends are in Holland. They will be glad. They are in great need. They are twice obligated to you and to Mr. Teverson—once for their lives and again for their property."

"Don't let them even mention it," Ward said dryly, "Teverson's cut of the proceeds releases them from all obligation. I'll have word of the other stuff in a few days. It's in good hands."

"I am confident of that to the utmost," breathed the little man.

The transaction was completed in a matter-of-fact small office to Rondalvo's entire satisfaction. Afterward he begged of Ward, "How may I find you? There is no way, and there is more business perhaps. I have many friends, here and abroad, and there is so much difficulty to help them in their problems."

Ward was first impelled to refuse any contact, but then thought of the treasures in Beecher's hands. If anything happened to Teverson and himself, Rondalvo was to be cut off from any knowledge of them. He gave Rondalvo Hymie Holtz's address.

"Inquire for us there. Holtz may not be able to get in immediate touch with us, but I'll be in frequent contact with him. He is to be trusted, but must not be told the nature of the job."

Leaving Rondalvo beaming and bowing in the drizzle, Ward traveled downtown to the Customs House. There he learned from his old friend named Dan that no such names as Kondar and Stuban were to be found in the alien permit files.

"Not many Berengarian names in the files at all, Dex. I guess they're a pretty clannish people, and stay at home. What do you expect to do about these fellows?"

WARD SHRUGGED. "I'M not sure of doing anything. These names may be in error. The whole thing may be perfectly regular. I'll take it easy, and let you know later."

Ward departed, and on Broadway entered a cigar store and telephoned Stephanie. Her man Carl answered, reporting her gone out. He also reported a message from Teverson. Everything was all right and going smoothly.

Stephanie, Ward recalled, had mentioned the possibility of calling today on one of her countrymen and fellow conspirators, to pick up the latest secret advices from the homeland and to forward messages of her own plans. She had delayed her own return overlong; history was in the making across the ocean. Ward could understand the tension, the suspense, upon her and her friends these fateful days. Nevertheless he growled a little to himself, worrying about her sorties through the town alone, and finding cold comfort in the thought of how soon they were to cease.

On impulse, spurred by a kind of morbid curiosity, Ward rode uptown to Yorkville and hunted up the address Hymie Holtz had given him as the residence of the pair, Kondar and Stuban. It was a cheap walk-up flat building in a section poor but reputable enough. He found the names in the entry, exactly as given, and after a moment's debate, rang the bell. He had no plan; he knew they could not possibly recognize him, and any excuse would serve him for a moment's chance to size the men up.

But no excuse was required. There was no answer to the bell. He abandoned the project, and after pacing the wet and gloomy streets a while, dropped into a neighborhood picture house to kill time in the sheltering darkness.

It was mid-afternoon when Ward walked into Hymie Holtz's office. That affable citizen was occupied with nothing more pressing than the perusal of a racing sheet.

"No, no business this time," Ward told him. "Merely a social call. I'm engaged in keeping out of trouble. Don't mind the feet on the desk—I'll take them down if a customer turns up."

"No bonds you sell today, eh?" Hymie said dryly.

"I've retired on my winnings." Ward lighted a cigarette. "Hymie, who usually makes the pinch in the case of an alien illegally resident in this country?"

"Immigration officers. Labor Department."

"How quickly do they operate?"

"That depends on the importance of the person and if he's likely to try a get-away. If it's criminal, any cop will oblige."

"I see. I'd like to use your phone, If you don't mind."

He called Brooklyn again. There was no news. He hung up with a wry expression. There had been no news in more than two hours.

Half a dozen times Ward interrupted a desultory conversation with Hymie Holtz to repeat the phone call. Each time Stephanie's henchman Carl answered, and each time his report was identical.

There was no further word either from Stephanie or Teverson.

Ward's feet no longer rested confidently on Hymie's desk. "Something is seriously wrong," he finally told the man at the other end. "You'll have to try to trace Madame Gorda, Carl. Put through phone calls to all her Berengarian friends you know, and find out all you can about her movements."

Calling back ten minutes later, he learned that none of Stephanie's people had any news of her. Ward swore vividly, full of alarm. This now amounted to sinister mystery. Teverson's silence intensified the gravity of the situation. The coincidence meant only trouble, inexplicable and dread.

WARD OFFERED THE keenly curious and somewhat crestfallen Hymie Holtz no explanation, but muttered thanks for the hospitality, and departed. He walked down Sixth Avenue, racking his brain for a reasonable explanation for this dread development. He could think of none but disaster.

The bleak day was falling early, smothered in mist and fog. It was certain to be a night made expressly for mystery—and, Ward came to resolve, for decisive, reckless action, if no reassuring word turned up. There were a few measures yet within his power. For one, there was Duff Garry's downtown on Calvert Street. It was the nearest source of positive news.

He continued downtown steadily, awaiting the oncoming dusk.

It was at Fourteenth Street that Ward finally gave recognition to something that had been knocking on his consciousness, demanding admittance.

The newsstands he had passed were almost all covered from the rain, and the headlines on the stacked evening papers were out of sight. But a man reading a paper in a cafeteria window, another in a doorway, had held up headlines half exposed. One such headline caught his eye—and held it fixedly.

He could not see the entire legend. But he saw one word, one thrilling, shouting word. That word was—BERENGARIA!

Ward ran for a newsstand, bought three papers, and ducked into a bar, where he examined the news over a drink. Chills of triumph raced along his spine. Though his name was nowhere in the dispatches, he was part and parcel of the tremendous news they all contained.

Berengaria was in revolt!

The correspondents fairly stuttered their astonishment and feverish reaction to such totally unexpected news. The victorious rebels, of the former prime minister's party, had sprung up out of nowhere in the center of the capital, and seized the national palace and the parliament house.

Other parties, incredibly armed with machine rifles, had pounced on the radio stations, the newspaper offices, military posts. The peasantry was rising, and an army, also reported to be heavily armed, was marching upon the capital to occupy it and maintain peace until the national police could be purged and reorganized.

The dictator and his aides and a small detachment of secret police were under siege in a fortified villa in a suburb, with no one hastening to their aid. His party was paralyzed, and the provinces were stunned, supine.

The coup d'etat was incomplete at the time of filing of

the dispatches, but the revolt seemed overwhelmingly a success. The former prime minister, its inspired leader, was said to be speeding from one point of action to another, maintaining iron command and everywhere receiving the devoted, almost hysterical acclaim of the citizenry.

One point baffled every correspondent. The country was known to have been ruthlessly stripped of arms. The moderate party now so suddenly in power was long known to have possessed none. None had come illegally into the land through any traceable channel. Only the terrifying fire power of their modern weapons had enabled the small scattered bands of revolutionists to achieve their amazing successes against great odds. All Europe on the morrow, although sympathetic by a large majority, would stand in wonder of this miracle. Whence had come these magic unknown arms?

Ward folded the papers with emotion stirring deeply within him. Many emotions, both bright and black, commingled and confused. He rejoiced for the freedom of a people, and was glad that so tremendous a blow for freedom had been almost bloodless. He had made this possible, and secretly put his mark upon history. And yet…

And yet if it had failed, these patriots destroyed, their leader struck down in death—Stephanie would have belonged to him alone. She would have had no other place, no preferred person on earth to turn to but him.

He put the thought violently aside, and went out again into the rain, and resumed his grim march upon Calvert Street.

Once again, before committing himself to this ultimate resolve, Ward phoned Brooklyn. There was still no word. Ward told Carl the news of Berengaria, to the latter's incredulous, desperate gratitude, inarticulate but very real, and then took the plunge.

18

STEPHANIE DISAPPEARS

HE MADE HIS way into the neighborhood and to the street behind Duff Garry's without meeting trouble. He proceeded without hindrance, exactly as he had done before, to make his way to the dreary yards at the rear of Garry's.

For a time he waited in Garry's yard, watching, listening, feeling for whatever menace might lie before him. He could discover no sign of the presence of men in the rear of the place. He went to the door, gingerly turned the knob, and let himself into the bare little hallway.

He slid his .45 into a side pocket, the safety off.

From the front came the steady sound of voices in the tavern. Ward listened at the doors of the rooms off the hallway, opened them, found them empty. He went forward to the door leading to the tavern, paused there a moment, on edge with keen awareness both of the recklessness of this move and its dire necessity.

Then he opened the door abruptly. His darting gaze swept the busy bar and crowded tables and fastened on the heavy figure of Duff Garry standing just inside the bar enclosure.

He said, "Garry!"

Duff Garry alone turned around to look. His face quivered with the secret shock of recognition. Ward waited. Garry glanced about, moistened his full lips, and then hastened to the rear. He closed the door quickly as he joined Ward.

"Man, what are you doing in my place? You know it's suicide."

"I want some information, Garry."

"There's nothing I can tell you. I never set foot from here. They come here, but they tell me nothing, man."

"Then you'll damned well find out for me! Where's Teverson?"

The solid frame wilted a little. "Have they got him again?"

"Where is he?" Ward drew the .45, and tapped the man's chest with the muzzle. "You'll talk tonight, or I'll shut you up for all time, Garry!"

Garry backed against the wall. "Put up the rod, Ward; I'm not fighting you. Let's go in the back room and talk."

Ward looked at him with flinty gaze and then said, "All right. Lead the way."

Duff Garry's fear was an agonizing thing, and Ward soon saw that the man did not dissemble. He was a mere tool, fully aware of the danger in which he stood, helpless between two fires. In the room he talked with a rush of words, pleading that Ward believe in his ignorance of The Eel's plans or methods, his horror at Teverson's plight.

"I played square with Tev, Ward. But these killers put a knife to my throat and told me to come through, or else. There was little enough I could say; I didn't think it mattered. I admitted that Tev came here to meet the people he does business with. I admitted he lived at the Blassingame. That's all. But they've been hounding me for weeks, ever since The Eel got the tip somewhere that this was a good place to waylay Teverson. You know all that has happened. I hadn't a hand in any of it."

"Were you playing square the first night I came here?"

"I was, so help me! I didn't know until after that gun battle what I was let in for. I've been in hell, man."

"Hm," said Ward. "What's back of this campaign of extermination, anyway? Isn't this world big enough for Koerner and Teverson?"

"It isn't half big enough. Heaven and hell ain't big enough. Don't you know why? I overheard it at the bar one night. Just the mention of it, that is. Tev killed The Eel's brother a year ago. They were trying to hijack Tev, I suppose. It was somewhere on the Hoboken docks. Tev got clear away after the shooting, but The Eel's young brother was shot dead. There's been hell to pay ever since, quiet and out of sight. It's blood feud—and this Eel man got his start in the Mediterranean ports, where they push a blood feud to the very end."

"What kind of start?"

"Smuggling, waterfront piracy. All his rackets. I don't know any facts, I only know the odds and ends I've picked up since the gang pushed in on me and took my place over. The Eel himself never comes here; I've never seen him. I haven't the least notion of where he keeps himself. I think from hints I've heard that he's an escaped convict from Devil's Island, and that his whole mob is organized along the lines of the great bandit outfits that turn up every now and then everywhere over southern Europe. He's as vicious as the very devil, and twice as cunning."

WELL, ALL THIS makes him human, anyway," said Ward. "I was beginning to have doubts. But it doesn't help me with what I'm here for. How am I going to find Teverson?"

Garry threw up his hands in despair. "So help me, I can't tell you that!"

"How do you make contact with them? Haven't you an address, a phone number, a name?"

"Nothing. They ask of me only that I shut my mouth."

Ward stared at the big man for a moment. Ward's face was neither pleasant nor merciful to see. He suddenly gripped Garry's coat front.

"I think you're lying, Garry. You are a yellow double-crossing dog, and my only contact with The Eel. I'm going to get something out of you if I have,to gouge it out with this gun muzzle. How can I locate Teverson?"

Garry's face was gray. "I swear I'd tell you if I knew!"

Ward cursed, holding him helpless. *"Then find out!"*

Garry clutched convulsively at Ward's arm. "Listen! Here's somebody. Ward!"

The door outside leading from the tavern into the hall-way opened and closed. Footsteps sounded deliberately.

Ward sprang to the wall alongside the door. Opening inward, the door would conceal him. He said, "Play ball for your life, Garry."

The door opened. Invisible to Ward, someone paused on the threshold, then said in a soft snarl, "What the hell's the matter with you?"

Garry stood looking at the newcomer with desperate eyes. He tried to speak, failed.

The newcomer stepped into the room. He was a squat, powerful figure of a man, dark, mustached, heavy jowled; he was suspicious and threatening. "They said you popped back in here in a sudden lather as I got out of the cab outside. What's wrong? Can't you talk?"

Silently Ward moved.

Garry's eyes did not swing toward Ward, nevertheless something in them warned the squat man. He pivoted suddenly, snarling, pulling his gun.

Ward leaped, striking. The heavy .45 caught the man on the side of the head above the temple. It finished him. He sprawled in convulsive unconsciousness to the floor.

Ward stood poised above the man. He listened, then said, "Are there any others?"

"I don't know," Garry said. "There generally is. Don't wait to see. I didn't even know he was here. Get out, get out the way you came. They'll kill me for this, Ward!"

Ward snorted. "Tell them the truth. They'll be too astonished at that to do anything. And deliver a message for me, addressed to The Eel himself. Tell him that I have a bit of blood feud of my own for him to pay off. And that I'm on my way right now to settle in person."

"Tell him *what?* What do you mean?"

"Precisely what I said. And God help anybody in the way!"

Ward stepped into the hall, listened an instant, and fled out the rear door into the misty darkness, full of a frustrate fury.

Safely out of the neighborhood of Garry's tavern, Ward again telephoned to Brooklyn. Carl was now a little unstrung by his vigil.

"No one calls," he reported vehemently. "I have sat by the telephone. There is trouble, sure. Madame Gorda would not do this."

"We've got to go looking for her, Carl," Ward said. "Get out the boat and come pick me up."

"But the boat must be here. There will be need if she calls, if Mr. Teverson calls."

"There's a greater need on the river! We can't sit waiting. You bring the boat and a couple of guns and meet me. I'll wait at Madden's Point near the Queensboro Bridge. You know it? Right! Watch for my signal. Get over in a hurry!"

MADDEN'S POINT WAS a small rocky projection in Manhattan's backbone into the swift currents of the East River. The shore line here was a soaring rocky bluff, isolating the point below in lonely darkness reached by a long flight of wooden stairs. A small clubhouse and dock had been erected at the water's edge by the youth of the neighborhood who swam here in summertime.

Ward groped his way down to the dock, where the night and the fog enclosed him in a solitude eerie and chill and depressing. Even the never silent voice of the great city was muted by the great gray blanket of mist that had rolled in from the Atlantic. An occasional river craft crept by, fog horn hoarsely blowing, a briefly visible wraith of dim illumination quickly swallowed by the night.

Inaction was difficult enough to endure, but the train of thought that beset Ward in this gloomy place and hour was a torment. Uncertainty and misgiving and dread assailed him, and doubt of his ability to face what lay ahead. To fight was one thing; to fight alone, facing an invisible and relentless enemy, was quite another. He thought of Tever-

*"Stick 'em up!
And freeze!"*

son and the kind of madness that had owned the man, and he understood it better now. He thought of Stephanie, consecrated to some unknown end too obscure to be divined, gallant in her resignation, loyal even in the footsteps of death. He thought of himself, blown on the winds of chance.

And then he swore and strove to think of nothing but this hour, this grim moment. Life was not to question, but to serve. To serve with all the ardor and strength in a man's possession, without flinching, without asking favor, with calm acceptance of its inscrutable rewards. Life was struggle unending.

The deep purring of the engine as Carl brought the boat feeling its way along the shore was a sound intensely welcome. A brief exchange of flashed signals, and the craft nosed in to the dock. They were off instantly, crossing the channel to the Welfare Island side, making northward at

Ward's direction. The breeze that struck their faces as they peered into the night was moist to saturation.

"Where we go now?" Carl demanded, towering, grim.

"Make for Fort Schuyler on the Sound. I'll direct you when we get there."

"And what you do there?"

"I'm entering a house where I'll not be welcome. But I'll not be expected, either. I'll have to play my luck. Want to come along?"

"You think Madame Gorda is maybe there?"

"That's the gamble."

"Then I go along."

It was a suspenseful and dangerous journey. The small patch of water visible close about them looked slick, greasy, ominous. A couple of times the mournful bellowing of a fog horn, increasing in volume directly ahead, rasped their nerves with its menace, until the looming mass of light of a huge freighter suddenly appeared, to be narrowly avoided. They listened for buoys, and reckoned directions blindly, and kept steadily traveling. There was peril for any small craft in these main traveled waters, but there was also sanctuary for the hunted in this limbo of fog.

They pressed on.

It was as much by desperate luck as cunning that Ward finally oriented himself along that dark shore and identified the dock and beach of the sinister old estate. The motor, slowed and muffled, made little noise. Quietly he cruised the adjoining waters, searching, but he found no trace of the schooner at anchor. It had been moved again.

"Well, we'd better get this over with," he said. He could

not help dreading a little what lay ahead. "Ready for shore, Carl? Got a gun along?"

Carl patted his body with grim suggestiveness. "I have better for this work. My knife. It is not new to this."

They tied up the boat to the dock and went up toward the silent, lonely house.

19

DARK DUNGEONS

NO LIGHT SHOWED anywhere tonight either, nor was there other sound or sign of occupation. Ward led the way with infinite caution over the grounds. He passed by the house, located the sunken garden.

The secret door admitted them readily to the concrete tunnel. Once inside, Ward flashed his light.

"Carl, you stay here. If I get in trouble, duck out of here."

"So then I do what?"

"Go to the police. If Tev and I are both knocked over, however it may happen, there'll be nothing left but a job for the cops. They'll do us no harm then. And they may possibly find Stephanie."

Carl grunted his disapproval of the place assigned him, but did not argue.

Ward walked the length of the tunnel. The tiny beam of his pocket light traveled over the iron door at the far end. It was old, but in good condition. It looked capable of withstanding a siege, but Ward, in reasoning out this invasion of the house, concluded two things: that no one here expected a siege, that no one expected an intrusion of any kind.

The secret of the house was regarded as secure.

Ward quenched the light. His fingertips explored the door, pressing it, testing it for solidity and treacherous noises. He gripped the heavy knob, turned it slowly. It gave. His heartbeat was a thunder in the silence.

The door opened on pitch darkness. Ward stood still, absorbing smell, sound, sensation. The presence of human beings somewhere within that darkness was a palpable thing, but he could feel, too, that walls, doors, lay between. He flashed the light.

The room before him was bare, concrete-walled. It was a mere entry to the house. Three light doors led from it. Ward stepped in, fixed the door in mind, and quenched the light again. He gripped his gun, and tried the nearest door with caution. It opened silently on darkness.

A sensation of horror slowly crept over Ward as he analyzed the sensations that came to him out of that further darkness. The living nearness of humans. But like something corrupt. A dank, even foul dampness, dungeon-like. A feeling of misery and confinement. He listened, and heard the breathing of men, many men, all plainly sleeping. Grim curiosity compelled him; he flashed the light into the place.

It was a place of confinement, of concrete and steel bars forming cages. There were inmates in the cages. He quickly let the flash die without attempting closer inspection. He closed the door silently, and his skin crawled a little. Here was mystery, fantastic and horrible.

Groping to the next door, Ward opened it. A flight of stairs, visible in reflected light from above, led to an upper floor. The stairs were narrow, old, obviously part of the original construction of the house, but sturdy and clean.

A faint murmur of voices came from somewhere above, desultory, unsuspicious.

Ward quickly disposed of the third door, which opened on a matter-of-fact cellar containing a furnace and old household gear. He returned to the second, and mounted above, treading carefully. No sound betrayed him; the stairs were enduringly built by careful hands.

A door, left open, led from the upper landing. Ward paused there to study his situation. His nerves were taut, hard, icy cold. The door, which was almost absurdly small, opened on a kind of hall, carpeted, clean, bright. Somewhere off the hall were gathered the men whose voices now were clearer. There were three, by the sound.

Ward stepped into the hall. The reason for the smallness of the door was now clear. It was one of a series of wooden panels in the wall—a secret door long ago installed. Quickly Ward walked on the soft carpet toward the voices. They came from a room opening on the left.

There was no longer time for hesitation. It was the moment for the ultimate, dread gamble, staking all on a single play. These men were alone; Ward could feel it. He walked to the open doorway, both guns out and leveled on the room.

"Stick 'em up! High! And freeze!"

The three, sprawled about a table littered with cards, money and liquor glasses, were dazed. They obeyed, but incredulously, all instinct for resistance numbed by the patent impossibility of this disaster. They were youngish, hard faced, dark featured all. Liquor had glazed their eyes a little. They were in shirt sleeves. They had been overtaken in a moment of complete relaxation.

WARD STUDIED THEM, studied the room, planning. All his senses strained to catch a hint of danger, of being caught off guard. One of the trio suddenly cursed. "It's that new gun of Teverson's!" he exclaimed in horror.

"Shut your mouth!" snapped another.

Ward stepped into the room. "You'll talk when I tell you to. Meanwhile, you'll all keep shut. Now stand up. Hands high. Walk to that wall and shove your faces at it. That's it. Now stand perfectly still till I'm finished with you."

The helpless, but now murderously raging trio occupied Ward's painstaking attentions for the next five minutes. He found only two small revolvers on them; they had laid aside their major armament. He tied their hands behind them with knotted handkerchiefs, working fast. Neckties served to bind their ankles. He sat them against the wall in a row. They were safe for a time.

Without wasting breath in questioning the three at this point, Ward hastened below, brought Carl back and had him mount guard over the prisoners. He ranged swiftly through the house, finding it a place of elaborate deception—a luxurious dwelling establishment and hide-out lurking behind the dingy, deserted looking exterior.

Upstairs were living quarters, all empty. He failed to find what he most of all desired—what he had already despaired of finding here. The thing had been too easy. Teverson and Stephanie would never have been so lightly guarded. If they were captive, it was in some other place.

Ward descended the cellar. He entered the dungeon-like section a little gingerly, watchful of traps. He found the light and switched it on. Then one appraising glance around, and he understood the gruesome mystery.

The place contained a dozen or so prisoners. Most were Chinese, although one was a Negro, and a couple white, foreign.

Ward said, "Any of you speak English?"

"I do," said the Negro, coming doubtfully to the bars.

"Who are you? What are you doing here?"

White eyeballs rolled. "I don't think—I doubt I dare answer questions, sir."

"Why not?" Ward snapped. "You're British, aren't you? West Indian?"

"I am."

"I get it. I've heard of you fellows. You're being smuggled in, aren't you?"

The man looked hopeless. "That's right. We were being brought in. But the men want more money. May I ask who you are, sir?"

Ward grunted. "Call me a friend in disguise. I can't turn you loose now, but I'll have you out of here in a hurry."

And he left them forthwith, although the Negro, fearful of worse things to come, begged for enlightenment.

Ward had heard of the pathetic victims of this modern day slavery, blundering wanderers who for one reason or another found the doors of America barred to them, and who resorted to guile to gain entry. Smugglers, contracting to bring them in secretly for nominal sums, betrayed them and held them for ransoms extorted not only from the victims, but also their families and friends. They had no redress in law. They were utterly helpless.

Ward, for all his desperation, his chagrin at the hollowness of his catch; had some satisfaction. That pathetic slave pen doomed this sinister house. Its location and its elaborate secrecy were explained. Both the police and the Immigration men would be grimly pleased to share its secrets.

WARD RETURNED TO his three captives above. He stood over them broodingly debating. They were tough and they were defiant. They would be hard to break. Broken they could be without fail, given time. But time was the last thing he could spare them.

One snarled softly, "Well, so what? What do you expect to do with us now?"

"It breaks my heart," said Ward, cold, hard of tone. "But? I think you're going into Long Island Sound."

They studied him, narrow-eyed. One said, "How?"

"With a load of old iron tied to you. I can't keep you. I certainly won't leave you here. You embarrass me. I've got to get rid of you."

They stared. And they were shaken. This man, with his terrible matter-of-factness, was not unknown to them. They knew his cold ferocity. And they sensed an invulnerability, a godlike finality about him, that passed their understanding. Terror came into a room with him, and death remained after him.

Ward spoke to Carl. "You'll find that front door open. Start moving them down to the boat."

Grimly Carl advanced on the trio. He reached to catch a hold on one, and the fellow cursed and kicked out with hobbled feet.

Carl dodged, and like a flash a long, heavy bladed knife whipped out, and Carl had the blade against the man's throat. The man did not move, and there were sudden beads of perspiration on his pallid forehead.

Carl said, "I waste no time. You choose which, eh?"

Ward stood imperturbably waiting.

"Okay," gasped the captive. "Take that thing away!"

Carl grunted, restored the knife to its sheath against his lean body, and hauled the prisoner erect and over his shoulder without an effort. He stalked from the room, while the eyes of the other two followed.

One of the pair began to curse in an unknown *patois*. Ward said, "Shut up! It won't pay you to force any unnecessary unpleasantness."

The fellow subsided. Carl returned after depositing his first burden outside the door, selected the second and removed him.

The third suddenly turned sick. His face wore a greenish pallor. "Wait a minute, don't do it, pal! Don't! I can't go like this!"

"Sorry!" curtly.

"Give me a chance, pal. What do you want? You got me, you can have anything you want, anything I got."

"What have you got?"

"My life—anything; I'll talk—I'll help you."

Ward looked at him, considering. "Well... one wouldn't be too much trouble. I might consider a deal."

When Carl stalked in a third time, Ward said, "Leave this one a moment. I'll have a talk with him. You can go ahead and fix up the other two."

CARL FLASHED AN opaque glance at Ward in which Ward saw complete understanding. Ward kicked up a chair and sat facing the prisoner.

"We'll have to settle this fast. First of all, where's the schooner tonight?"

"Foot of Ailanthus Street."

"Your boss, The Eel?"

"He's aboard. They got some kind of a rush job on tonight. The fog—they always work, this weather. The whole mob is downtown."

The floodgates were open, and the fellow talked. The tale he told was a sordid one of stealthy violence and furtive thievery, of piracy and terrorization as a policy along all the vast waterfront of the city. Its details little interested Ward at this moment, but he bided his time. He was concerned with the strength of the gang, which only Jules Koerner knew to the full, with the activities of the schooner, which by its respectability of appearance had served so well for a blind.

The fellow verified Duff Garry's theory of The Eel's insane hatred of Teverson. Teverson had the gang baffled for a long time with his activities. They had systematically ferreted out his secret. The Eel had first been wary, then envious, and finally covetous. The shooting of The Eel's brother had followed. From then on it was blood feud.

Certain rapacious members of the gang had thought it much smarter to blackmail Teverson, or absorb him, for his success was evident. But The Eel's hatred never waned. Only Teverson's elusiveness saved him. And persistence was defeating him, tireless, ferret-like persistence.

Ward heard the man out, and then began shooting questions at him. They were veiled, careful questions, admitting nothing, but hoping for much. He garnered further facts. The night's rush job at the foot of Ailanthus Street was a smuggling operation. Stephanie Gorda was a name without significance—to this member of the gang, at least. The gang had no clue as to Teverson's hiding place after his flight from the South Street house. A number of key places along the waterfront were kept under constant watch, in the certainty that Teverson would eventually be forced to show himself.

And last—The Eel. The man was originally from Monaco, half French, half Italian. The name Jules Koerner was pure fiction. He had terrorized the waterfront of Marseilles for a while, until apprehended, sent to French Guiana for life. There he had escaped, made his way north to America.

Only a man of sheer evil genius could have lived through it all, for he was—a cripple.

One leg was shriveled.

Enormous physical development in his torso and shoulders compensated somewhat, but his main reliance was his uncanny brain. He ruled from hiding, and ruled by fear. His brother, his only kin on earth, had joined him as soon as he had established himself in New York, along with a few other one time associates, although most of his men were American born or American bred renegades. And that was all the story.

Ward was silent. And Ward came face to face with the final fact. This man knew nothing of Teverson's disappearance, nothing of Stephanie's. The essential mystery remained unsolved, and the dread unrelieved.

Ward paced the floor, the brute rage in him unappeased. He snapped, "Where are the keys to those cells down below?"

"Leo—one of the other boys keeps them."

WARD STRODE OUT to the front door, outside which Carl stood grim vigil over the helpless pair. He instructed Carl to take all three to the cellar, and to lock them up in the cells. Then he ranged through the house until he found a telephone. He called Police Headquarters. His conversation was brief and to the point, reporting his sinister discoveries in a certain old mansion house on Throgg's Neck, describing the location, urging immediate investigation in force both by the City and Federal authorities.

There was a certain hard satisfaction in that. But there was none in his next call. As ever, endlessly, it was to Brooklyn, and he learned from one of Carl's fellows only that the silence of Teverson and Stephanie remained unbroken.

They did not linger. Ward urged Carl to speed the boat as they thrust forth into the fog. He damned the fog for delaying them, and they grimly blessed it for its concealment and protection. He would have much need of it this night.

They sped, reckless of the night. They raced to southward, downriver. An infrequent light, a moaning whistle, a buoy feebly clanging, guided them.

Carl said, "We go another place now?"

"We do. It'll be a tougher place than the last. Still with me?"

The man's voice was even, stoic. "I am sworn to her service. Where she goes, there I follow. It is until death,"

Ward thought, good man! He said, "We'll accomplish more alive than dead. Don't get too reckless."

"Where do we go?"

"On a schooner. You know where Ailanthus Street is?"

"Ailanthus? I think to remember."

"It's downtown East River. A bad neighborhood. There's

an open dock there. You'll have to cut the motor and drift under her bows."

"And you think this time is where is Madame Gorda?"

"It's got to be."

"Good. So we find her."

Nearing Ailanthus Street, they crept through the fog alongshore. The lights of moored barges and tugs, of occasional street lamps, shone fitfully, guiding them. The tide was just past the turn, gently ebbing. They shut down the motor entirely, drifting. Ward perched on the bows with the boat hook ready; Carl took an emergency oar and sculled at the stern. They made way slowly, in effective control, passing a dim, unreal panorama of shadows along the shore. Traveling with the current, they made not a sound in the dead water.

"Watch it now," Ward said finally. "Ailanthus just ahead."

Carl grunted. They crossed a space of open water where the line of docks receded into invisibility. Ahead, Ward knew, a long open pier projected at Ailanthus. He peered into the fog. No light shone, nothing was visible.

Then he heard sounds, muffled. Tread of feet on timber, hushed tense voices, a curse. A soft thudding of wood… of wooden boxes, it was to be surmised, lifted and dropped. There was a feeling of furtive haste, of danger and audacious enterprise.

Then, looming abruptly, the graceful outline of a ghostly vessel, and the long shadow of a wharf.

They drifted soundlessly under the bows. Ward fended with the boat hook, let the little craft come to rest gently under the bowsprit next the pilings of the pier. He groped in darkness, line in hand, threw a double half hitch around one spile. He went aft to Carl, treading silently.

"Hold her here. I'm going aboard."

"I go also," Carl said.

"I want you ready for a getaway. Stay here."

CARL ONLY GRUNTED. Ward took the boat hook, thrust on the pier, and moved the boat directly beneath the bowsprit. He sprang up, and climbed, monkey-like, over the peak of the vessel.

From that vantage Ward studied the deck. It seemed larger, viewed here, than he had imagined. Further aft, a flashlight winked, revealing the dim figures of men moving on the deck. He could not make out their number or their occupation.

On this unfamiliar ground, a direct attack was out of the question. Ward intensely regretted that he had not the machine gun along, that he could not challenge and invite battle, shielded by the benign mist. The sight, so close, so fearful, of these men who had wrought such evil, filled his soul with a gusty passion. He spun the automatic on his finger, nervously pent up, thinking, devising.

He moved. He crowded the starboard rail, in the shadow of the dock. He advanced slowly, one careful step at a time. He made out a dull glow of light amidships. He was puzzled; then recognized it for a half open saloon port.

He crept toward it. Then, nearing the port, he heard a step, quick, cat-like. He whirled, cursing silently. But too late—an unseen hand caught his gun wrist, held it in a grip of iron, the automatic impotently pointed upward. A gun muzzle jolted into his stomach. A huge figure loomed; the man breathed into his face.

"Don't move. No sound, rat. Who are you?"

Ward was rigid. Thought spun like pinwheels, coping with this. The man had waited in ambush. Alongside the foremast. A posted guard.

"Who in hell do you think you are, you damn fool?"

The man hesitated, then snarled, "Cut the eyewash! Talk, or I'll give you this load in the belly. Where'd you come from?"

"Off the dock. Where in hell else?"

But the man tensed; the grip tightened. He cursed softly. "I know you. Damn you, I've heard *you* talk before! Drop the rod!"

Ward remained rigid. The gun muzzle dug into his flesh. Desperately, cold with the clammy chill of last extremity, he shifted his weight to one foot. A single chance. To drop like a plummet to the deck, to kick up the gun…

The man barked, *"Drop the rod, or I'm shooting!"*

Then all at once the man uttered a single shuddering, gurgling gasp—and went unaccountably limp. He let go the grip, the gun fell away. He leaned slowly forward, putting all his weight on Ward. Ward caught him, dumbstruck.

A voice beyond hissed, "Is all right! You put him down quietly."

It was Carl. Ward lowered the heavy body. He felt a warm wetness on his hand. He lay the body in the scuppers and wiped his hand on the cloth of the coat. The body did not stir.

Carl said grimly, "I follow you. I think is better."

It was the soul of a savage warrior speaking, brooking no

denial. Ward had none to offer now. He said curtly, "You win. Come along. But not too close."

"What you do here this time?"

"I'm looking for Stephanie and Teverson, dammit! I'll do what seems best when I locate them."

"What if there is no sign. You cannot fight. Too many men."

Ward paused, then said grimly, "All the better. They won't miss one if we take one for a ride. We can find out from him."

"How?"

"We can tow him on the end of a line for a mile or so out in the river. When we pull him back aboard he'll talk your ear off. Wait and we'll see. You trail after me."

It was impossible to make out the exact lay-out of the vessel, but Ward judged this midships structure to house the main cabin. It was more like a yacht than a cargo boat. Aft, the stir of activity continued, overflowed onto the dock, with only an occasional dart of light, revealing nothing. The mutter of voices was indistinguishable.

20

IN DARKEST WATERS

THE SMALL CABIN port opened on the ship's saloon, where a light glowed dimly. It was partly open. Sensing emptiness within, Ward shoved it further open. He saw no one. Aftwards was the companion; various doors, all closed, led to other quarters. He called Carl.

"I think the whole gang's aft. I'm going below. Keep watch. Tap on the housing if there's danger."

His blood raced with the opportunity, slender as it seemed. Carl remained on the spot.

Ward crept along the housing to the companionway.

Once below, Ward rushed the search. The cabin, rather handsomely appointed, offered nothing by way of clue. He opened a door. Somebody's quarters, dark. Another. Additional quarters. Then an office. A pantry. A store room. A passage, leading, by the vague oily smell, somewhere toward the engines.

No least sign of Stephanie or Teverson anywhere!

He stood nonplussed, in a torment of frustration and defeat.

A sudden shout overhead electrified him. Three quick taps sounded on the housing. There was a pounding of many feet. Ward leaped for the companion—and came to a halt on the first step. They were upon the housing, at the companion.

He hurled himself at the nearest door, and inside. He was in one of the staterooms. He stood still in the darkness, ear to the door, cursing over and over in profanity that was half prayer. Above him a tumult of stamping and pounding raged, without single sound of a voice. There had been only that solitary shout of alarm. He waited.

Abruptly the violent noises ended. There was a more deliberate shuffling. Then someone came down the companion. They all came down. There were sharp, grim commands, and a snarling, and apparently a great shoving and crowding. There was a feeling of hatred and brute violence.

And Ward understood. Carl was taken prisoner.

There began then what was for Ward an inescapable horror. Carl, by his mere presence on the schooner, was doomed. They did not know who he was, nor why he was here, and they meant to learn, yet no possible explanation could save him. They questioned him, and he, knowing his fate, defied them grimly, unshaken and unshakable. They threatened him, and he laughed, deep in his throat, tauntingly. Death could not daunt him; he knew his countrymen had triumphed, knew that Ward had somehow escaped, knew that he still had it in his power to confound them.

"You bet I come alone," Ward heard him tell them. "You bet I kill that fellow with my knife. You think is hard to do these things? Ho! I fight three of you, alone. I have bad luck. I cannot fight twenty. Is bad luck, I tell you no more."

A DEEP VOICE, strident, commanding, suggestive of great lungs and vocal chords, with a mongrel Latin accent, snarled softly, "Who sent you? What you come here for, pig?"

"Is very foggy night. I came for steal what I can steal."

"You lie!

"Then why you ask me? You already know?"

A powerful fist struck the table. "You tell me or, name of Judas, I give you the garrote! You know the garrote?"

"I do not care for the garrote. You can do nothing to me. I come here myself. I come by the dock. All the men are busy aft. I can steal something easy. I have the bad luck— one man walks by the dock and sees me before I see him. I tell no more."

A member of the gang came below from the deck to report. "No sign of anybody else, boss. There's a speed-boat tied up under the bows. Empty. And Mike up there's finished; no hope."

There was a silence for a moment. Ward, the hot reck-lessness of a creature at bay brewing in him, ached to hear the next words.

"A speedboat!" purred the deep voice. That velvet purring was a cruel sound, a terror-striking sound. "You come to steal trash in speedboats, eh, pig? It wouldn't be you come by orders of a man by name of Teverson?" No answer.

The voice went on, "Since there is no talk, I think I know what to do. I put you back in the speedboat and send you into the river. I send you home. With a souvenir. You will be wearing the iron collar. Pietro—the garrote!"

Ward gripped the brass knob of the door. He froze to it for an instant. Then he turned it, slowly. The door came open on the merest crack, and he could view a section of the outer room.

At the table opposite him they were forcibly seating the sardonic Carl in a chair. Two men held him fast. He sat facing Ward. Ward could not be sure, but be suspected the presence of a sudden, veiled smile on Carl's face, and a slight shaking of his head. His face, usually so imperturbable, was alive, aflame with a kind of intense zeal.

Ward could not yet see the man with the deep voice. He did not try—yet. He watched Carl.

A Satanic little man, beady eyed, expressionless, brought a heavy iron instrument, a thing like a large micrometer or vise. He slid the collarlike loop about Carl's neck. At the rear, just at the top of the spine, was a heavy handscrew. When turned, that screw would press inexorably against the spine, and press increasingly, cruelly, lethally, as it was turned. It would finally pierce the vertebra. It was a crude adaptation of the instrument of execution frequently used both in Cuba and China, one of the most fiendish ever devised.

The little man glanced down the table.

"Begin!" hissed the voice. There was tense silence.

The little man turned the screw. The slack caught up, the pressure began. Carl's neck strained against the collar. He grinned, and it was a ghastly grin of triumph, not quite human.

The voice, gloating and fiendish, purred huskily, "You suffer. You have only begun, my stubborn one. You will pray for death. It is slow and terrible to come. You will tell us some things, no?"

With agonized lips, Carl spat at the speaker. Another man leaned over and calmly struck Carl across the face with the back of his hand.

AT THAT, INCONTINENT with hatred, Ward opened the door. He flipped up the automatic and shot the satanic little man between the eyes. He caught one glimpse through the crowd of the deep voiced man at the end of the table—a black-haired, leather complected man of forty odd, bull-like of torso, powerful and evil of porcine face—and with his second shot in a split second, shattered the electric light overhead. In the darkness he leaped at the nearest man, felled him with one hammerlike blow of the automatic, and sprang over the collapsing body onto the table.

The small inclosed space of the pitch dark saloon was instantly filled with a boiling madness. Most of them had not even glimpsed Ward before the light was extinguished, knew only that Death was among them, terrible, unknown. They knew not whom to fear, to fight. They broke for the open, and jammed in the narrow companion, cursing, yelling superstitious supplication.

Ward, crouching, moved down the table. Feeling blindly, he sought its end—or contact with the man at its end. Upon that man's immediate extinction life wholly depended. Someone screamed a sudden hideous scream, and there was a rip fire of shots. Oddly, in that milling frenzy, no man brushed him, or collided. All avoided the table, crowded the walls. Ward listened, tried to catch in the bedlam the sound, the unforgettable sound, of the voice of the huge man, Jules Koerner, The Eel.

Then, instead of the voice, Ward's ear caught in an instant's lull, the snap of a door closing just ahead. He found the edge of the table, slid from it, rushed toward the further corner whence came that sound. Nothing obstructed him. He met a door, found the knob, prayed fiercely he was not mistaken, and opened the door.

"Who is there?" It was the voice of The Eel.

Ward fired. He slammed the door after him, charged.

In that faintest light from the discharge of the automatic, Ward half saw, half sensed, the disappearance of The Eel through a further door in the narrow stateroom. He was upon it as it slammed, fired twice through it, threw it open.

Beyond was blackest darkness—and silence.

Ward hesitated, lowered himself in a compact crouch. The panic in the room behind him was already subsiding as someone took command, yelling for light and order. The terrible need for haste was like fire through Ward's every nerve, the need for the immediate judgment of death. The Eel had the tremendous advantage of knowing this darkness intimately. He had slithered away to this lair in no cowardice or desertion, but in soundly tactical retreat, considering his physical handicap, the overwhelming numbers left behind. Here the handicap was Ward's.

The silence ahead was unbroken.

Ward felt for his pocket light, careful to make no sound. Somewhere ahead The Eel waited. Surely he had no gun on him, had not had time to get one, or he would have fired. Ward's very flesh was cold, chill with uncertainty. Ward cowered against one side of the doorway, extended the flashlight across to the other side. He flashed it on— caught one glimpse of the vast gloomy interior of a kind of tweendecks—and a mountain fell on him, crushing him.

It was The Eel. He had waited just to one side of the

door. Waited until his pursuer betrayed himself, and then thrown himself massively on him, cursing, gloating.

WARD STRUGGLED, RESISTED instinctively, half dazed, yet fully conscious of the terrible menace atop him. The darkness blinded both, aided Ward. The fearful hands of The Eel sought his face, his throat. The man grunted, cursed in a paroxysm of blood lust.

Ward's gun was gone, lost in that crashing collapse over the threshold. He fought back with bare hands. He gripped the great body, braced himself against the door jamb, and came partly to his feet, raising the other from the floor. Then he let himself topple forward into the tweendecks. Both crashed together, were torn apart, groped madly, and rolled over the deck flooring, fighting without skill or thought, maddened primeval adversaries.

"You die!" grunted Koerner. "Now you die!"

The great hands were at Ward's throat. Ward thrust stiff extended fingers straight at that voice, at that face. He struck home, and the man screamed with the agony of an injured eye, abandoning his hold and recoiling.

Ward was after him like a flash. They clawed, jockeyed for holds, fending each other's murderous hands. Koerner's strength was beyond anything in Ward's experience; here, threshing on the deck, the man was under no handicap. Only the trained skill years in Ward's background saved him from that overwhelming brute power. It was inhuman.

Then, in a breath, the threshing ceased. Now Koerner beat the timbers of the deck flooring with his hands, but both bodies were still. Ward had the oxlike head in an unbreakable lock with his right arm. The Eel cried out with the unendurable pain.

There was perspiration, icy cold, on Ward's face. There was a suspension of all emotion in his soul. He knew what was coming. So did Koerner. And both knew that there was no evading and no compromise. Ward's entire body drew on all its strength for the task.

There was a space of dreadful quiet in the darkness. Not silence, for there was the sound of gasping, tortured breathing, the sound of muffled guttural outcries, rising in terror, the sound of Ward's teeth grinding from the terrific compression of his jaw. There was a moment when time stood still. Then there was an abrupt sound oddly like the sudden cracking of a wooden broomstick. It was the end.

Ward staggered a little when he got up. He felt a peculiar numbed feeling, as if drunk. He felt for his pocket light, found it missing. He groped for a match, struck it, and made for the stateroom threshold. He searched, and picked up the scattered flashlight and the automatic.

From the door he sent the narrow beam of the light across the deck. It came to rest on the giant figure of The Eel lying motionless, lying in a twisted, most peculiar manner.

Ward swore softly. There was no emotion in his voice.

Then abruptly he bethought himself of the gang in the saloon, aft of him. He switched off the light, took a grip on the gun, and stepped to the door to listen.

It was very quiet beyond the door. It was an unnatural quiet. He tried to account for it, for the absence of pursuit in here.

The door suddenly swung wide open, and a dazzling glare of light blinded Ward. He half raised the automatic, froze still. In the light he spied the lean hungry muzzle of a machine gun, trained on him.

"Drop the gat!" a voice commanded crisply.

Ward dropped it, benumbed.

The voice said, "Who are you?"

Something began to click in Ward's consciousness. "Who wants to know?"

"Bureau of Narcotics, Treasury Department, friend." The man stepped into the room, flashing the light on his own face, young, lean, grimly efficient. "And I reckon you're this Ward fellow they're kicking up about."

WARD GAPED A little. "Kicking up? Sure, I'm Ward. Who's kicking up?"

"A highly agitated guy by the name of Teverson. You'll find him up on deck, along with more cops, detectives and assorted citizens than you ever saw together before."

Ward tore past him on the run.

Teverson was there, restrained almost by force from a personal search of the vessel, when Ward flew out on deck. The deck swarmed with a confusion of men, and automobile headlights on the dock flooded it with illumination.

There were several machine guns in sight, and a number of police uniforms, and along the inner rail of the boat was ranging a sullen, defeated rank of very cowed prisoners.

"Ward!" Teverson yelled. "You're all right?"

"Where's Stephanie?" Ward demanded.

"Safe and sound. Back on the street in a car with Doc Beecher and Hymie Holtz. They wouldn't let them in here. My God, it's a relief to see you."

Ward stared, blank of face. "How in hell—?"

"It's quite a story. Yours comes first. I want you to meet an old friend. Inspector Dineen—this is Dex Ward."

Ward felt a little tense, like a fighter squaring off, as he gripped the officer's hand.

Dineen was big, gray mustached, blue eyed and poker faced. He stared, and drawled, "So you're the murder fugitive?"

"Am I?" Ward said warily.

There was a twinkle in the blue eyes, cunning and calculating. "I'd have nailed you flat if I could have laid my hands on you. For information, if nothing more serious. And you'd have boarded at the Tombs too. Dexter Ward was a badly wanted man."

"You mean—under that name?"

"The same, boy. We traced the prints."

Ward moistened his lips. "And so?"

Dineen chuckled; his affability was the kind that wore steel beneath it. "Well, maybe I didn't look too hard for you. Don't count too much on all a copper says. That Spider fellow actually pulled through that night, and we're holding him for grand jury for murder. He's just out of the hospital. You're clear on that job."

"Then... why did you publish those prints of mine?"

"Because I didn't want to publish the prints of the real murderer. I wanted that story kept on ice. It was a managing editor's idea. Your prints came in handy, and I threw him a bone. I held back the others because I had a hunch that that Webb man was an Eel gang lieutenant, and we've managed to keep the arrest practically under cover. I even told you he was dead. We've been all in the dark about this

Eel thing. I learned more tonight than in six months. I'm glad we got him."

"*You* got him?" Ward snorted, and could not down, for an instant, the hot ire that rose in him. Then all at once it did not matter. "Well, I'm sorry to disappoint you, Inspector. But I'm afraid you haven't got him."

Alarm sharpened Dineen's gaze. "We haven't?"

"No. I got him first. You'll find what's left of him down there below."

DINEEN STARED, THEN made a dash for the companion. The lean young Federal man was just coming up. He wore a wry look.

"Somebody done spoiled a hot conviction for some young prosecutor," he drawled. "The big heat is lying down there all messed up, with his face in the small of his back or thereabouts."

Dineen swore in angry disappointment.

Ward said to Teverson, "Where's Carl? He was with me."

"Carl? I dunno."

Ward frowned, swore urgently, made suddenly for the companion. The Federal man barred the way.

"Not now, pal. Not till all's checked up."

"I had a friend down there with me. I don't see him up here."

"Won't do any good to go down now, I'm afraid. What's your friend look like?"

Ward told him.

The agent said, "Tall thin fellow?" Slowly he shook his head. "Too late, Ward. I'm sorry. I looked them over. Three of them, under the table. Your friend is shot dead. The fellow alongside him has a knife clean through him."

Ward sagged a little. He felt weary. He did not say anything. He turned and walked back to Teverson.

"Get me out of here, Tev."

Teverson frowned, shook his head in doubt. "They'll want us around."

"Get me out of here! Let's go sit in the car. I can't stand the very smell of this place any longer."

Teverson consulted Inspector Dineen about it. The Inspector debated the matter, eyes hard and bright and realistic. "You're under arrest, Ward, do you realize that? Automatically. You've just committed a homicide."

Ward smiled sardonically, humorlessly. He shrugged.

Dineen said, "You've got a gun on you now, haven't you?"

"I have." He still had the little .25.

"Then hand it over."

Ward looked at him. It was necessary to think that over. It was a little hard to realize that the everlasting menace had actually ended. He breathed deeply, and surrendered the automatic.

"I'll let you sit in the car if you'll give me your word you will stay there," Dineen said grimly. "By rights, you should be locked up immediately. We have grounds for suspicion of other homicides. What your disposition will be, I can't say now. You'd better not talk too much."

"I won't."

"I'll let you know a bit later how you stand."

21

STEPHANIE'S GRIEF

THE INSPECTOR TOOK them shoreward, passed them by the police line at the foot of the pier. Half a dozen cars were parked on a dark, empty factory street.

A car door opened as they approached, and Stephanie got out, to stand for an instant, peering uncertainly, and then to come running.

"Dex!" she said, and all her terror and ache of relief, all of a myriad emotions, were in the one word.

"Everything's all right, Stephanie." He smiled a little.

She walked beside him back to the car. Teverson gave her the details of what had happened. They got in, and Ward greeted Hymie and the doctor absently. The two men watched him, silent. Ward sat back and closed his eyes.

"I don't have to mention the big news, Stephanie?" he murmured.

"No, of course I know it.... It's wonderful news." Yet somehow, without any failure to appreciate the news— the news from Berangaria—the tone did not live up to the words.

Ward said, "Stephanie... I'm sorry. Carl got his."

"He is—dead?"

"He went out fighting. He saved my life. He tried to save yours the only way he knew."

She sat very still. She could not speak. In the darkness he squeezed her hand.

Ward said, "Now it's somebody else's turn. Let me in on it. What in hell happened?"

They told him an extraordinary story. That day Dex Ward had wrought more mightily than he dreamed. The many threads of his separate making had come together to weave a remarkable pattern, the finished design of which was tonight's combined raid and rescue party. Quite apart from the police and homicide angle, the rescue angle—the Narcotics Bureau men were unexpectedly exulting in the capture of half a million dollars' worth of refined dope hidden in the center of jars of cold cream and standing now on the pier in small packing cases where it had been in process of unloading.

Two small trucks were part of the haul. The stuff had been lying aboard the schooner for days, it was believed, in transfer from a Levantine freighter, waiting just such a night as this for delivery ashore safe from any prying eye.

Thus was explained to Ward the sounds he had heard as he crept up the schooner, the activity he had dimly seen on her deck.

"Swell break for the Narcotic boys," he said. "But how did they know? For that matter, how did you know I was here?"

Hymie Holtz chuckled and said, "A little punk we find up on Throgg's Neck tells us all about it. You, the dope, the schooner, the works."

"Throgg's Neck? You mean the punk I turned the heat on?"

"He said he already done some talking, and maybe he better do some more and stand in right with one side anyway."

"But what took you to Throgg's Neck?"

Teverson explained that. A matter of logical deduction. Ward had been looking for the two missing members of their corporation. He had demanded the use of the boat and Carl's assistance. That could mean but one thing, knowing Ward so well. Throgg's Neck. A two man rescue.

They had raced up to the Neck, where their hunch was confirmed. They found a police raid already in progress. They combined forces. On the information supplied by the terrified "punk," the Bureau of Narcotics had next been invited to join. The whole combination had descended on the schooner only a comparatively few minutes ago—to find bedlam loose on pier and vessel, and all resistance disorganized. They had simply walked up and taken possession without even a serious challenge.

Ward smiled a little grimly at that. "The whole gang had their nerves all shot by the time you came along, I imagine. They must have thought it all part of the same party. I'd go so far as to say that there's no doubt that a number of cops and agents are deeply indebted to Carl this minute for the fact that they're alive and walking around. That gang was organized to give serious battle."

Stephanie murmured, "And indebted to you, Dex. Behind all this is your planning and your risking."

Tev added, "And not a little bit of his fighting."

THE EVENT THAT day which had precipitated all the

night's unholy violence, the disappearance of Stephanie and Teverson, was so simply explained that Ward mentally kicked himself for his density.

He had practically stumbled over it, and had not recognized it.

Stephanie and Teverson had been waylaid and spirited off by the secret agents Kondar and Stuban!

"That pair is not so dumb as we thought," said Hymie Holtz. "They went to another detective agency, after I told them it was no onions, and naturally the other agency finds out all that I found, only this time the boys get their money's worth. The taxi driver tells them where he dropped you that night—at a pier in Brooklyn. They don't understand, but they go there and hang around, trying to figure it out. And so they run into Miss Gorda and Mr. Teverson coming home, and stick them up and off they go to Yorkville for a long heart to heart talk and a murder or two maybe if you ain't careful."

"They were desperate," said Stephanie. "They had accomplished nothing on this mission, and there was alarmed word the last few days from Berengaria that arms were on the way from America. They did not know how, and they had orders to find out. It was death if they failed. The only place they knew to find me was that pier. They waited, and Tev and I walked right Into their arms. They had a car, and they had guns, and I knew it was useless to make resistance. We went with them. They took us to their flat, where they asked me many questions." She laughed, with defiant scorn. "They are fools! They learn nothing from me."

"They were just beginning to air a few ideas about torture," Teverson added dryly. "They meant business too.

It took rather a sizeable load off my mind when the Doc here and Hymie Holtz strolled in and broke up the party— one by the door and the other by the fire escape."

Ward, in the midst of his almost bewildered reception of these amazing details, turned over in his mind one clear hard fact gleaned from the lot. Stephanie and Teverson—together—going home. That would be about noon. Together, unannounced and unexplained. He made no comment.

"If you'll explain how Hymie and the Doc happened to stroll in on this party," he drawled, "and made it add up to sound good sense, I'll believe in Santa Claus from here on."

Dr. Beecher chortled softly. After a lifetime, adventure had finally visited him, and at least a decade had dropped from the total of the years. "I telephoned to Mr. Holtz and pressed him to keep his promise to come have tea this very day. I was uneasy, my boy, and I found that Mr. Holtz was equally so. You were constrained and full of some apprehension you would not explain. Mr. Holtz and I talked it over, and decided it must be these two Berengarian agents you had on your mind. Mr. Holtz had good reason to think so."

"Why not?" said Hymie. "You tell me once they are assassins. You ask me this morning about arresting illegal aliens. You call on the telephone and Miss Gorda is not home or reported, so you go rushing out all steamed up. What should I think? I come to a conclusion it wouldn't be a bad idea if the Doctor and I should go calling on these fellows and have a look."

"It was I who entered by the fire escape," Beecher interposed. "We quite surprised them."

"So we have a good look, and we find just what I thought," went on Hymie, "and we think everything is fixed up—and next comes the disappearance of Dex Ward. It was too much!"

TEVERSON SAID, "AND so it was my turn, at that point, and I thought it a good idea to take a look in there up at Throgg's Neck. I didn't know the exact place, and we stumbled right into the arms of the cops. It was a bit embarrassing, to say the least. When I got wind of all the information they were collecting, I decided it was time for showdown. I got permission to phone Dineen, and had a heart to heart talk. With The Eel on the skids, it was possible at last to play ball with the coppers. So he organized this raid, and here we are—out from behind the eight ball at last!"

"What's happened to Kondar and Stuban in the meantime?" Ward inquired.

"If they're not on Ellis Island, they're on the ferry going over, by this time," said Teverson. "There'll be no charges. They'll have their hands full when they face the new government at home."

"I think maybe there will be a firing squad," Stephanie said grimly.

Ward winced mentally. Words of death and the thought of death were things of which his very soul was sick. He asked her, "Have you had word from your father yet, Stephanie?"

"No word." There was worry in her voice. "But he is so busy, I know. He will exhaust himself. And there is still such danger. I should be with him...."

There was a silence.

It was very late, and there had been a great coming

and going of patrol wagons, police officials, newspaper-men, before Inspector Dineen sought them out with his report. A breeze was rising and the fog had thinned. He had Ward and Teverson walk up the quiet street with him for a private talk.

"Teverson, I'm not telling just how much I know about your business on the waterfront," he said. "It's phony enough, and I'm warning you. But we know that dope shipment was a frame-up—the junk wasn't even the genuine! So no police charges will be pressed for the present. I know yours was not the dirty game this Koerner played, and you'll find the police willing to give any man a break that keeps his hands clean."

"I've played ball with you before, Inspector," said Teverson. "I will again. This Eel thing was outside the law."

"It was a dog fight, and I know how you feel. Now as for you, Ward," he said grimly. "The same pretty much applies, with one very important difference. You're a man with a reputation in town now. It's a bad one—very bad from the police angle. It'll get you in trouble sure, and give us plenty to worry about. I could put you away to cool for a good stretch in Sing Sing. But I know your hands are clean enough too, and I'm willing to strike a trade."

"What kind of trade?" said Ward.

"Leave town for a while. Clear out and stay out. Save us the worry, and we'll save you the stretch."

Ward reflected, and his thoughts were bitter. "This is my town. Inspector. I didn't create this trouble."

"That's exactly my point. No more will you create all the trouble ahead that I'm thinking about. You see, trouble's my business, boy. I know how hard it is to put an end to it, once into it. No man with the fighting reputation you've made will be allowed to live long without it. You can take your choice."

"All right," said Ward. "You win."

Released from official custody, they all drove west to a late restaurant on 14th Street and had breakfast. Conversation was desultory, they were all weary after the fury of the day and the long let-down of the night's waiting. Ward and Stephanie sat together, but the little they had to say was quiet, impersonal. Impersonal, although each was aware that this might well be their last meal together.

A NEWSBOY PASSED among the tables, discreetly crying his wares. He came to their table, to hold up a paper hopefully. The sheet bore heavy black headlines.

EX-PREMIER KILLED IN FIGHTING AS
COUNTER REVOLT IS CRUSHED.

Stephanie stared, her face drained of color. Then she screamed, snatched the paper from the boy. She devoured the subheads, the story lead, the account of a battle and of one man who had fallen in it. Slowly the paper lowered. She looked at the others. The look on her face was one of numbed sensation, of a spirit stunned.

"Gentlemen," said she, faltering, "my father—my father is dead."

But looking at her, looking grimly and pityingly, they knew she spoke with unbelief.

They took Stephanie out of the restaurant like one walking in a trance, docile to their wishes, and unaware of them.

They got into the car and drove back eastward to the river. Ward sat beside her, silent, watching her.

The others glanced at the news, discussed it in low tones.

A desperate counter revolution had broken out in Berengaria, the ousted party briefly rallying and attempting to retake the capital at any cost. The movement lacked any substantial popular support, and failed.

Order was soon restored, but in the brisk and bloody fighting the leader of the new government had fallen in a street engagement.

The frenzy of grief sweeping the nation assured him a hero's memory, and was the most complete indorsement of his cause that could be conceived. He had fallen, but his cause was safe, enduringly redeemed.

He himself belonged now neither to his party nor his friends nor to his daughter, but to the legends of his valiant land, forever.

When they got out of the car again, Ward said, "Tev, stay with the car. Let me take her in the boat alone. I'll see you tomorrow."

Teverson looked at him an instant. "All right. Look after her. Don't leave her."

"Thanks. I won't."

Teverson gave his arm a squeeze. The others walked with Stephanie a little ahead. "You're the only one can help her now, Dex. And there's something I want you to know. I'm entirely to blame for the kidnaping today. I called her from New York and asked her to come over and meet me for a talk alone. She did. I was taking her home afterward when it happened."

"Yes?"

"We had quite a talk. It didn't do any good, but I thought I'd try. I tried to make her see that she should stay here and stick with you, Dex."

A weight was lifted suddenly from Dex Ward's heart.

TEVERSON WENT ON, a little grimly, "I still think you belong together. You're made that way, made for each other. I'm not. I started to tell you something last night when they opened up on us with that gas. It was this. That I'm a lone wolf, and nothing can change me. I've prospered at it all my life. Even when we ran together I was chiefly running alone, and you never got to know me down deep. I belonged to myself alone, and gave nothing of myself to a soul on earth, man or woman. Until this year. When I crossed myself by getting involved with both of you. A woman. And a friend."

"Then you did take a dive for her?"

"Like a brick chimney. And I hit bottom in just as many pieces. I didn't intend to, but I let myself *need* that woman. I let myself need that friend. Too much. And before my eyes I saw you both go straight to each other. I was in need, and alone. It was poison to me, Dex. It ruined me. I hated you both for my own weakness.

"I get it, I get it."

"It will explain a lot to you, perhaps. Why the bottom fell out of me. I wasn't yellow; I was empty. I'm glad you went for each other. It's not my way. With women or with men—not to that extent of need. My way is to run alone. I'm going back to it."

Ward looked at Teverson. "Good luck, Tev. We may run different paths, but they'll never be far apart."

"They needn't be. We can still be friends. All three…

Make her stick, Dex. If I were you I'd never let her get away."

Ward smiled a little, a grave and earnest but assured and understanding smile. "I don't intend to. She has no reason now to turn me away. I'm going back to Berengaria with her. She doesn't know it yet, but she'll soon hear about it. We'll come back to New York together along about the time Dineen judges I'm sufficiently cooled off to be allowed at large."

"I'll be waiting."

The police were still on guard at the foot of Ailanthus Street, but Ward and Stephanie were readily passed and allowed access to their boat. As they walked out on the pier, Ward looked back. Teverson still stood in the lonely pocket of illumination cast by a street lamp. He stood brooding and alone, watching them. Watching them out of his life….

Visibility had greatly increased on the harbor. The dark waters were iridescent with diffused reflected light. Ward eased the little craft into the tide. He did not hurry. Stephanie sat alongside, silent, cowering into herself, into a kind of numb, blinded denial of life and its terrible realities.

Ward said, "Stephanie…."

She did not answer. He put one arm around her. She was rigid, but after a moment she leaned over close against him.

"Stephanie, my darling!"

She gave a convulsive movement, and all at once was lost, racked, helpless in a storm of profoundest grief. She wept with desperation and heartbreak, with all her soul and life and body.

She clutched, clung to him, in terrible need of him.

"Oh, Dex, keep me, hold me now!"

Ward held her and patted her and smiled a little, with a strange gentleness, looking down at her. It was good that she wept and spent her grief. He guided the boat steadily, and did not speak again. There would be time for talking. He held her close....

And presently the fair winds swept the harbor and the fog was gone, and the dawn came over the dark waters and was a majestic glory and a hopeful promise after the gloom of fog and night. And Ward, watching it, saw in it the answer to all life.

Beside him, her head on his shoulder, Stephanie slept. And the boat crept on over the dark waters into the clear new day.